DD'S UMBRELLA

TRANSLATED BY

DD'S UMBRELLA
HWANG JUNGEUN

E. YAEWON

TILTED AXIS PRESS

CONTENTS

d 07

There Is Nothing that Needs to Be Said 117

1

d saw lightning strike as the five o'clock assembly was about to begin. The school day over, d had remained behind in the classroom when out of nowhere a pale, slender forearm reached through the dusty black windowsill and touched the floor. d noticed a burnt smell and upon creeping closer saw that the spot was singed.

d was crouched over this mark when dd's voice drifted in from the door. What are you doing?

Come have a look at this, d said as they beckoned.

dd walked over.

Look. d pointed at the floor. Struck by lightning. Just now.

d reached out and traced the mark with their hand. dd followed suit.

See how only this spot feels warm?

Incredible.

Their heads nearly touching, d and dd ran their fingers over the marred spot again, then got to their feet. d drew the fluttering curtains aside to peer out the window. dd walked over to look. The sky was threatening rain. Kids stood in clusters in the schoolyard, backs weighed down by heavy packs; a handful of teachers were dotted around. Everybody was very still and facing the same direction. Clothes flapped and clung in

10   dd's Umbrella

the relentless wind. The pledge signalling the close of assembly
ended. d and dd watched as everyone scattered, heading off in
various directions. Closing the window, they made their way
outside. They'd crossed the schoolyard and were headed out
the gates when the rain started falling. d opened an umbrella.
dd held out half a bar of chocolate. They walked together,
sharing the chocolate and the umbrella.

They reached d's house. Bye, d said from the doorway of
the dark woodworking shop.

dd continued on home under d's umbrella.

d remembers the day, remembers seeing the bolt of lightning
strike in front of their eyes. It was an extraordinary thing to
witness, unprecedented and as yet unmatched. d remembers
the exact shape of the mark, how it resembled a small mouth
with an upturned corner. They had assumed the pressure of
their fingers would gradually rub it out, but it hadn't. d had
looked and looked, completely entranced. Had there been
someone else in the room? Possibly. But this is the extent of
what d remembers. Apparently the two of them had chatted as
they headed home under the same umbrella, but d has no
memory of this either. They are gripped with remorse, feeling
somehow at fault for misplacing the memory. d has recurring
dreams about the day even now.

Then it happened.

d reached for a towel to dry their face, only to let it go —
lose hold of it, in fact. This was just before nine o'clock on a
Wednesday night. The second hand on the bathroom clock
was ticking. Soapy water pooled in the sink while d stood
barefoot on the tiled floor. What d had grabbed and hurriedly

let go of was a regular old towel, plain and mundane; something that was and always had been to hand. Every day d dried their face and neck on that towel before replacing it on the rack or dropping it in the laundry basket. An ivory-coloured cotton towel, somewhat stiff and threadbare from repeated washing and drying, devoid of distinguishing patterns, marks, or embroidered initials. This banal object had, out of nowhere, developed a palpable warmth, as if the fabric itself was emitting heat.

The bathroom door was open towards the darkened kitchen. Walking past the kitchen table, d knocked off a desk calendar. Groping to retrieve it, d noticed that the thirteen sheets of thick cardboard paper and tightly spaced spiral binding running along their upper edge were warm to the touch. d set the calendar down and placed a hand on the table. Also warm. It didn't stop there: various items of furniture, plates and cutlery, glass objects, handles, all seemed to give off a moderate heat. That was the day d realised that objects that should feel cooler than air were now in fact warmer, as if they'd developed their own body heat or morphed into some uncategorised subset of living organisms. d found the sensation intolerable, and as far as they could help it, avoided touching all but the most necessary of items. But surely the world can't have changed so drastically overnight, d thought, which must mean the change is in me.

I must have grown colder.

d's father Yi Seung-geun was a woodworker. Yi Seung-geun, his wife Goh Gyeongja, and d lived in the attic room above his woodworking shop. After removing their shoes at the door, the family climbed three cement steps in the corner to reach the

12 dd's Umbrella

single room where all three slept and ate. There was a wardrobe, a low table, and a Braun-tube television. A kitchenette had been fitted to one wall but the room was windowless, and anytime Goh Gyeongja made soup or steamed meat, the strong, savoury vapours wafted through the room and down into the shop. The wood pile was steeped in the smell of soup, rice, and banchan topped with red chilli powder, while the room they shared was fragrant with wood scent. Years before, teachers and classmates had turned to d for answers when they wanted to know about trees for the sole reason that d lived in a woodworking shop, but in truth d knew next to nothing about trees. You don't find trees in a woodworking shop — wood and lumber were what filled up a woodworking shop, not trees. Timber sawn and cut into boards and planks, then cut a second time and set aside until selected, altered in shape and form, and stuck fast with either nails or hide glue; sticks and smaller fragments of wood stripped of bark: these were not trees, certainly they looked nothing like a tree. Next door there was a small shop selling kids' stationary and toys — thin sheets of faded craft paper and rubber balloons grey with dust — and a butcher's that left darkened, dry meats in their display fridge. The woodworking shop was as cramped and tucked away as these two neighbouring shops, and as bereft of light, no matter the season or time of day. The air was sharp with sawdust, and stale wood pieces rotted and swelled in a sour heap.

Yi Seung-geun wasn't much of a woodworker. Sometimes people dropped by the shop to complain about the shoddy job he'd done. Having encountered more than a few dissatisfied customers over the years, Yi Seung-geun had developed an attitude that was polite, fawning, and apprehensive. When the

Hwang 13

inevitable occurred, he accused his clients of contriving to lower his fee. People are so predictable, so shamelessly transparent, he'd gripe, but even d could tell their pa's woodwork was mediocre. Yi Seung-geun produced objects that were neither meticulous nor well-proportioned, and fell woefully short of being practical or beautiful or original or even outlandish. d couldn't figure out why their pa didn't simply admit this; why instead of owning up to his lack of skill, he pretended otherwise. Yi Seung-geun never raised a hand to d, never complained about his wife's cooking, always finished his food, and wasn't at all interested in drinking or betting. Instead, he kept up a litany of his own importance, reciting how *his* woodwork kept the three of them fed and clothed and how this made his labour sacred. Makita, Hitachi, Lexon, and Bosch power tools, chisels, hammers, planes, folding saws and fret saws: with these Yi Seung-geun cut, drilled, shaved, and sanded, and the acoustics accompanying this work constituted, for d, the soundtrack of the day-to-day world.

The blurring of work and home space made it impossible for d to escape this harsh, jarring noise. d ate, napped, watched TV, and did their homework to its insistent track. The grating of the rotary saw cutting into wood was particularly gruesome. Sometimes, when there was no work to be done, the shop was quiet, but once the commotion resumed, which it inevitably did, d would sit in the dim family room with a pencil, either doing their homework or doodling, their ears growing hotter every minute, and remind themself, That rotating saw is what keeps me alive, the cost of woodwork that's neither honest nor pleasant to look at is what feeds and clothes me. Or they'd imagine sticking their little finger in the rotating disc-like blade of the saw and bide their time. Waiting for the moment when

14   dd's Umbrella

the blade, stained with their pa's blood, might splutter to a stop. Waiting for the moment their father would halt his sacrosanct work and the workshop would fall silent. Then, in shame and guilt, d would glare at their pa in a fit of rage — or ignore him out of a deep disenchantment. There was nothing d considered sacred. Their ears burned and echoed with the din of timber being shredded, thin sheets of metal being torn up, a rustling as though tiny lint balls were rolling around inside their ears. Whenever d found themself in a quiet place, they were keenly aware that the apparent absence of noise had nothing to do with stillness or silence. The remnants of sound and static were a permanent presence. d grew into a taciturn adult who found no pleasure in speech. The world was clamorous enough as it was.

d met dd again at a school reunion. It had been raining all day. As old friends emptied their glasses and made small talk, d's left knee suffered the inevitable spilled drink, but it wasn't anything tissues and time wouldn't take care of. d headed out around midnight, only to find their umbrella had disappeared from the stand by the entrance. dd, who happened to be standing next to d, offered their umbrella. Here, take mine.

That's okay.

No, I insist.

d tried to refuse, but dd mentioned that they'd once borrowed an umbrella from d and failed to return it. d had no memory of this. It was back in the day, dd said, we were only kids. Remember when we saw the lightning? d couldn't recall this either. The lightning, yes, but not dd. So you were there? d said, holding on to the umbrella and looking flustered. Eventually the two of them decided to share the umbrella and take a rather circuitous but manageable route that would first bring them to dd's house. d carried the umbrella. dd stepped in and out of the umbrella's orbit each time they came across a puddle. It bothered d to see dd's hair and face getting drenched in the rain.

Bye, dd said from the doorway of their house.

d waved and continued on home with dd's umbrella. The fabric was blue with a red camellia printed on it, and the handle was a deep chestnut. It looked clean, but the sheen on the handle suggested lengthy usage, and a couple of ribs had been patched up. d left the umbrella out on the enclosed balcony. Once dry, the umbrella was neatly folded away and left hanging on the frame of the balcony window, next to d's own umbrella. The balcony was where the laundry basket and the washing machine were kept, so that each day, as they stopped to throw dirty clothes in the hamper or to hang up freshly laundered clothes, d would spot dd's umbrella. How strange, d thought. Each time d glanced at it, the thing seemed to stare back at d. As though it weren't inert, a mere object, but was in fact a smaller version of dd — as though d had borrowed a part of dd and had left it hanging there.

d worked at the Food Production Center at Gimpo Airport, where waterproof workwear and gumboots were mandatory. With each arriving flight, carts brimming with food waste and discarded packaging were wheeled over to the centre, where the employees would sort out the trash and wash down the carts. At the end of each day, their pockets and hats were inspected for smuggled bottles of alcohol and food items from the meal trays. Then a bus took d home.

One day d heard the bus radio forecasting rain and, once home, picked up dd's umbrella and immediately set out again.

16   dd's Umbrella

dd was waiting in front of their house. The two chatted for a short while before saying goodbye. And that was how the umbrella vanished from d's balcony: by being returned. Every day d went on the balcony with the day's washing, but now, instead of the umbrella, an empty metal hook dangled above the window. How strange, d thought. It was gone, yet there was such a haunting sense of it still. The palpable presence of that absent object made d feel such a gaping emptiness inside that they had to laugh and say, This won't do. So they arranged to see dd again.

In dd, d had found their sacred object. dd was the words that must continue, the body that must remain intact. It was through encountering dd that d learned how sacred their own labour could be. How a person who has love could be beautiful, how one could, simply by finding an object of beauty, experience sadness and joy. The noise that filled the world and occasionally troubled d no longer irked. I want to be happy, d decided. I want to be happi*er*. The life d and dd shared was shoddy, exhausting, and lacking in many ways, but they had their private jokes, their shared laughter and sorrow, their clasped hands. Thumbs tracing knuckles, fingertips caressing napes and knotted shoulders; holding each other's perfectly small and ordinary ears, kissing each other's necks, helping with coat sleeves when the days turned chilly. I'll be happy, d thought. I'll be happy alongside dd's happiness.

d and dd lived in flat B02 at 505 Mok-2-dong in Yangcheongu, Seoul. The area was a world apart from the sprawling apartment complexes: here all the residences were either twenty-year-old multi-units or detached houses. Being right at the edge of Yangcheongu, one only had to cross the big road by the bus stop to find oneself in the next district, Gangseogu. The homes in Mok-2-dong were predominantly brick red and encircled by low, ageing walls. The front door of flat B02 was tall and heavy and had been fitted with a frosty pane at eye level. Stepping over the rusty threshold revealed an entryway about an ankle's depth lower than the ground outside, followed by a living room, a kitchen, a bathroom, and a bedroom all arranged single file and in that order, as on the horizontal space of a train. The B is there more for convenience's sake, the estate agent had said, as you can see it's not very deep, hardly qualifies as a semi-basement really, so in fact it's more a ground-floor flat? The inflection in his voice seemed to dispute this even as he declared it as fact. But the flat was located on a subtle incline, and from the front door to the bedroom one could trace a gradually declining, and definitely subterranean, slope. The wide bedroom window was level with the ground outside, so that side of the flat was definitely a semi-basement. But this flaw was not reflected in the rent. What swayed dd and d's decision in favour of the place was its being equidistant from their workplaces, and its nonetheless markedly lower price.

The renter, Kim Gwija, was an older woman who couldn't read or write. When the agent asked for her bank details, she seemed uneasy and said the tenants could always pay her directly, in fact she'd come and knock on their door, yes, she'd knock, like so, and all they'd have to do is open the door and hand her the money, they wouldn't even have to step outside. Right in here, she said, showing an upturned palm. Her hand looked small, pale. d looked at the hand waving inches from their face with alarm. Something about the woman's face seemed familiar, the cloying smile perhaps as she chattered on

18   dd's Umbrella

about this intrusive method of rent collection. d was irritated and offended, but decided the place itself would do.

dd had wanted a well-lit space and in this respect the flat failed to live up to their expectations, but they settled in well enough nonetheless. dd slept, ate, washed, got ready for work, came home after a day of work, watched films, listened to music, talked about getting a cat, collected small pots of succulents, spoke of a specific coat they wanted to get next winter, fretted about how watertight d's work boots were, caressed d, slept in late, worried about bills, had the occasional insomnia, was neither excessively hopeful nor excessively despairing, and generally acclimated to their life in the flat. dd would frequently cut their hand on the edges of curled-up wallpaper or on ancient door handles where the paint had peeled off, and oddly, on Sundays, and only on Sundays, muddy water would drip from the bathroom ceiling and trickle down the grooves in the tiled wall. During the months when the boiler was switched off, it wasn't uncommon for them to startle awake in the middle of the night because of the chill creeping up through the floor and the bedding.

It was on their way back to this room that dd was killed.

Hurled to their death.

d could not shake this thought. Other thoughts jostled in their head, but in the end this was what d kept coming back to. Hurled to death. Out of a packed bus. As though in the impact of the collision a delicate and merciless pair of tweezers had plucked then flung dd, and only dd, onto the hard road the two of them had walked together every day.

Since becoming aware of the dull heat that had seeped into most everyday objects, d had stopped leaving the flat. They stopped going to work, stopped making phone calls, barely ate and drank. Holed up, they proceeded to smash, shred, destroy, and trash the things around them. It was painstaking work and after a while d's hands started to burn from the heat. To dispel the sensation, d would scratch their head or rub their palms against their body as they worked. Sometimes there would be a knock on the door, a neighbour coming to complain about the rubbish piling up in the alley, but d carried on, ignoring the intrusion. Boxes were filled, items binned, yet more boxes filled. Everything d disposed of went on emitting its low-grade body heat like some strange living creature, and with every contact d felt sickened. But d couldn't leave them be, because they lied, these objects.

d had waited, perplexed, for a good long while. After all, most of dd's belongings were still there: the baseball cap they pulled on down to their ears when they had to rush out sat in the closet, the slippers were exactly as they had left them on the doormat, and even the cup of tea from that morning remained on the table, dark with the residual dregs. Inside the shoe cabinet the cherished umbrella stood, neatly folded, while in the bathroom the toothbrush with its flattened bristles and a bottle of half-full hair product waited, as did the desktop calendar on which dd had jotted down reminders, and the pillows and blankets carrying their smell. It really did look as if dd had only popped out for a minute. They must be out there somewhere and would be back, whether this evening or tomorrow morning or perhaps even in a few days' time, undoubtedly, they would return as if nothing had happened. But when exactly? Not now, not yet, but soon. Soon: that elusive moment teetering into the next, the next now. Every second d felt sure it was just about to happen, and every second

20   dd's Umbrella

found their hopes dashed. Objects were behind this illusion, this anticipation that only circled back as intensified loss and betrayal. In ridding the space of its things, d rid both this deception and its accompanying false sense of reality.

Take dd's brown shoes. There was no other pair in the world like them. They had stretched to fit the shape of dd's feet, their uppers creased and lined, their soles worn down in the manner of dd's gait. Boxing the shoes, d thought: Now they're in this box, they can't be in any other box. Since a single object can't be in two places at once. They're in here now, meaning they're not in there. What's here can't be there. At least that's how it is for inert matter, but as for the *wearer* of these shoes – well, people aren't quite the same as things and *can* exist both here and there. Didn't I read or hear that somewhere? That even when someone's gone, as long as there's another person who remembers them, it's like they're still here? Are they though? The hell they are. People are too similar to objects in that respect: once they're gone, they're gone. They no longer are, certainly not here. d carried on sorting in silence, emptying entire boxes out periodically and putting things back in. It occurred to d that the stuff that refused to be discarded required sending on to dd's family, but after a while they stopped being able to determine which items they themself should hold on to. But they kept going, working slowly and methodically, until everything had been binned or boxed. Four days of ferrying back and forth to the post office and d was able to send the boxed belongings on to dd's family. After the last of the boxes were delivered to the post office, d returned home. And remained there, in flat B02.

2

The house at 505 Mok-2-dong had a simple exterior wall covered in glazed dark red bricks, no decorative features, and was topped by blue roof tiles. Inside, it was divided into two basement units, two units at ground level, and a single unit on the second floor, and this last was where the elderly Kim Gwija lived. In the yard there was a flower bed made with soil Kim Gwija had gathered herself and a row of bricks, and that by now was full of salvias, cockscombs, cosmos, gardenias, crown daisies, and a still-young Korean cherry tree that bore yellow fruit. And poppies — these Kim Gwija had nurtured from the seeds she'd collected when a single plant sprouted up one day, out of the blue, in her yard. The poppy flowers were red or yellow or white with dark centres, and their single set of petals fell away to reveal olive-like seed pods.

The neighbourhood women came, parasols in hand, to look at Kim Gwija's poppies. So this is aengsok, is it? ... The best thing for bellyache and toothache and chest ache I tell you, it's the real thing... The stalk in the centre of the clumps of toothed blue-green foliage was extremely thin, and, once the flowers had fallen away, would dry as it stood, neither bending nor breaking. Kim Gwija jabbed at the unripe seed pods to collect the latex, and when the stalk and pod were both

22 dd's Umbrella

thoroughly dry, she uprooted the plants and bundled them for storage. The older women who gathered at Kim Gwija's drank decocted poppy water and lay in the yard, chatting and idling. d would receive rice cakes and persimmon punch from the women as they were wont to unroll their straw mats in the shade outside flat B02. Here, here, try this cake... Here, youngster, have a sip of this too won't you, boiled it myself with plenty of cinnamon, it's good and spicy and the best thing for your lungs... Kim Gwija and her visitors wore summer rayon and waved fans with boughs or vines inked on them as they extended these treats to d. Accepting the plates through their window, d noticed how the women's hands, one holding a plate and the other a fan, looked both soft and sinewy.

For as long as the sun was out the women lounged in the shade and discussed their children, the weather, their ever-decreasing appetite, how nobody made their own fermented pastes anymore — and the war. Kim Gwija spoke of how just yesterday afternoon the sound of sirens had broken her nap and, knowing it wasn't the day for civil defence drills, she'd assumed a real attack was imminent and had fallen to the ground wailing for her ma. It took a while for her to realise that the blaring came from a loudhailer on a passing flower truck. The women nodded and commiserated, spoke of all the times their hearts had dropped to their feet from the same mistaken assumption. Still, they said, their fears *had* been warranted that one time, hadn't they, and that told you they weren't entirely off the mark. This was in reference to the defection of Lieutenant Lee Woong-pyung on 25 February, 1983, and the chaos and commotion triggered by false reports that Incheon was under attack by North Korea.

At the time the women had been living either in Seoul or in Osan or Gwangju in the greater Seoul area, and upon first laying eyes on Lieutenant Lee Woong-pyung in the newspapers and on TV, they were astonished to discover how tall and handsome he was. For hadn't they always imagined people in the North, whether civilians or soldiers, to be underfed, underprivileged, and ugly — your typical commie puppets? But here was this North Korean army pilot in his sophisticated fighter jet, looking less like a member of a puppet army and more a man of attractive qualities, and that got one thinking, didn't it, that maybe the situation up there wasn't quite as puppety as they'd imagined... But these doubts were doused by remarks of how, at the end of the day, that handsome soldier *had* chosen to depart the North in his fighter plane and fly here nonstop, all in a bid for freedom, and wasn't that proof of how puppety the situation in fact was up there and how good and free things were here where we lived? Yes, yes, surely it was, they said in assent, eager to complement one another. Yes, but even so, we know, don't we, how the good and free here could with one instance of war, a day or even half-a-day's bombing, be reduced to nothing, end up as rubble and ashes. You may not realise this, young neighbour, but we *know*, know it in our core... Having experienced their first war at a young age, the women said they'd lived expecting, or not so much expecting as unconsciously dreading or intuiting, that a second war would break out in their lifetime; hence these sudden involuntary flashes when they would feel once more how the past was still very much present, which suggested that within themselves, that is, in their core, the war had never wholly ceased, not for a moment. So they heard air-raid sirens in a truck vendor's loudhailer and wondered if it was real or a dream...

24   dd's Umbrella

Listen, d heard one of the women say, the first time I saw people being slaughtered was in June of 1950, when they bombed Hangang Bridge. Back then I had a husband and two children. My husband was carrying one child on his shoulders, the other child was on my back, and we walked through the night with everyone, gripped in terror, carried forward by the surging crowd. But before we made it over the bridge, there was a loud *boom*, I fell flat on my face, and then I felt something slip and scatter over my hand. I managed to pick myself up but the tide of people kept coming, and I straggled on in a daze, my wits gone. It was unbelievably slippery underfoot, I kept stepping on something slimy as I walked. But I carried on walking and walking and walking, there wasn't time to look back in all that forward momentum. It was only when I'd crossed the river and reached the darkness on this side that I realised my husband was gone, and my eldest too. They must have crossed before me, I thought, they'll be somewhere up ahead. Going back was no longer a possibility as the bridge was destroyed, so I put my faith in these thoughts and stumbled on. Without food or water, my feet dragging, or else running like folk around me were doing. At one point someone spoke to me as they walked past, and that's when I realised I'd been carrying a dead child on my back. I opened up the blanket and saw the child's scalp was scorched. I could see the red bone of the skull. If I'd tied the blanket to my front, my back would have burnt off instead...

I may speak of this now, but I won't cry. I can't. Not then and not now. I was terrified, far too terrified to look back, all I could do was get away and by then I had nothing, I was all alone. Terrified and lonely to boot. So I met someone quick as I could and we started a family, had one daughter. That

Hwang 25

daughter has a daughter of her own now and they live, safe and sound, in Susaek. The grandchild takes after me. But the little one and her mama are always nagging me about my place, asking why I hoard all this stuff, that it looks a right mess, saying I need to get rid of the junk. What junk? They've all got their uses as far as I can see, but no, they say they're ashamed to run into my neighbours. You there, downstairs neighbour, why don't you name me two things you need? Because I have it all, whatever you need I have it. Will you have more rice cake? Well then, listen some more.

I kept going down the country. Days I walked, nights I slept standing, leaning against walls or trees so men couldn't climb on my belly, and once the sun came up, I would set off again on foot... Eventually I came to a small rural village where the other folk fleeing south had just begun to arrive, a place that hadn't seen the full extent of the war, where nothing had been razed or destroyed, not yet. It was so peaceful in fact that I thought my mind might finally quieten down. So there I was one afternoon, leaning against a wall and resting my eyes. The wall felt nice and cool and I was so exhausted, I began to think how wonderful it would be to drift into a never-ending sleep... But then I came to and noticed a gourd growing out of a cleft in the wall. A bottle gourd, still young and tender enough to eat. A lovely thing, pale and greenish. I grabbed at it and pulled. Not to eat it per se but because they were so pretty and tantalising like, the dozen or so hanging off the vine, and I simply had to pluck one. That was when a woman ran out of the house quick as lightning, screaming, Thief! Don't you steal our gourds, you thief woman! You bitch! and snatched it out of my hands. She didn't look a day older than me, her hair and face were all neat and proper, but her mouth went on spouting

26   dd's Umbrella

thief and *bitch*... And all at once, in all that bright daylight, I was overcome with so much sorrow and shame that my eyes started to water. I couldn't believe it. I was crying! I thought, I'm feeling *shame* of all things, well, well, so I *am* alive after all. Then I cried out of happiness and out of desolation. I have to live, I thought, I've made it this far, I might as well make it to the end. I knew it in my core. That sense of clarity, it came out of shame. Shame is what saved me. Now that I'm... how old? Let's see, one, two, three, four... Yes, it may well be a hundred years ago now, but in all those years it's stayed with me. That certainty in my core. My grandchild and daughter say I live in a scrapheap and they're ashamed of it, but I don't see the shame. I know shame, and this isn't it. It's natural, not shameful, for the living to be surrounded by life's scraps, natural and unavoidable...

As afternoon deepened the sun shifted, reshuffling light and shade. The rays fell upon the glass container of persimmon punch by Kim Gwija and her visitors' feet, and the refracted light found its way down to d's basement room to ripple against the wall. Watching the sparse net of that light, d thought of many things, and while d was deep in thought the women addressed nearly everything under the sun, from pollen and soil and war to salting and curing... Now and again, as they half-listened to these tales which seemed to be narrated at times by one voice and at other times by all three alternating voices, d wished that the women would either move away from the window or cease the movement of their spotted purple lips, only to realise they were hooked on the women's stories. In those moments, d wanted to hold tight to their words. But the memory of Kim Gwija offering to come to their door to collect rent and the jarring image of her pale, outstretched hand encroaching on their space would inevitably resurface, and d would shudder and wish the women would simply fuck off… And always there was a nauseatingly insistent urge to ask Kim Gwija if *her* possessions weren't warm too, and at times this urge would build and d would get worked up to the point of feeling violent, and wanting to scream, but even then their face remained, as they sat staring at the wall or at the veil of light dancing over the room, the very picture of serenity, and their eyes were, much like the women's, quiet, unfocused, and dull. And so, that summer, folded into the women's afternoon and existing as a mere outline like an empty, elongated sack, d watched as night crept in and the last of daylight daubed the walls in ever brighter hues, before yielding, incrementally, to the dark.

Where is the core.

d thought a person's core must be located at the jaw, because that was where their own pain was located.

d went entire days without opening their mouth, except for when they occasionally tasted blood and unsealed their lips. But no amount of prodding with their tongue revealed the source of the bleed, and it wasn't until later that d would realise the strain on their jaw and how tightly they'd been gritting their teeth. At night, as they lay staring at the dark with their lips clamped, the rest of their body seemed to fade away entirely until only the jaw remained. Then there was nothing to see or hear or miss or touch or be sad about, but only the chin, and the thought: This is it now, the chin is all there is. Then the core has to be in our jaws, ultimately. Because the core always comes last, it's always final. And if the jaw is last, the core has to be there too. Holding on, barely, between the

28 dd's Umbrella

upper and lower jaw — the one crushing the other, the whole thing stuck fast like magnets. In a mouth that feels like it's been bolted shut with a rusty lock, between the stiff tongue and the metallic saliva.

That was where the core was.

Kim Gwija had said that on 28 June, 1950, as she escaped off the Hangang Bridge, she'd glimpsed a slimy fragment underfoot in the afterglow of the bombing and recognised it as a human face. Though it was at most the size of half of a half of a bowl and stuck fast to a fragment of bone. The image haunted d. They couldn't stop thinking of the partial face that was once whole and attached to a skull; an intact, enclosed skull, with twenty-eight beautifully interlocking bones. A brain had resided inside that skull, a thinking, remembering, forgetting brain. A spherical brain. Brains are spherical because human skulls form a closed circle, a beautiful and firm round orb. This structural frame, and the solid interlocking of each skull according to a particular pattern, allows the brain to retain its round form. One might say its *life* form. Outside that structure the brain would simply uncoil like a jumble of rope, entirely defenceless. Each skull is one of a kind. When one skull breaks, the world loses what had existed singularly, its distinctive pattern undone. Irrevocably. But so what? d thought. What's a bit of loss in the scheme of things? Shit happens. It just does. It can and it does. dd's particular pattern, though, that must have been beautiful, joined in its own distinct way inside the face I could pick out in a sea of faces... Unique and therefore irretrievable, never to be held in this life. When that disappeared from my side, silently fell away to shatter on the black road, the road that had seethed and boiled with the falling rain... I wasn't holding on to dd, not the

Hwang 29

instant before, nor in the moment everything screeched to a stop on that road we'd walked together every day. But why wasn't I? What was the cause? Was it even a matter of causality?

Someone knocked on the door of B02, but d ignored it. The person returned the next day. d heard footsteps circling outside and, based on the sounds, thought it had to be men's shoes, the type with thin, hard soles and ample room either to the front or around the feet. And they were probably well polished; whether or not the wearer shined them every day, on this occasion at least they would be perfectly polished. d heard the front gate, heard the steps get closer. The window began to slide open. It creaked open a hair, then creaked open a bit more. d saw a man crouch down and peer inside. Behind the man stood Kim Gwija's flower bed. The poppies and salvias and cockscombs drooped, they hadn't been watered in days. d looked up at the man. Instead of demanding who he was, they attended to the man's face. The eyes and lips were clearly outlined and the hair neatly combed, but the crest of the nose curved to one side and gave an overall unruly impression. The man took his time giving both the semi-basement room and d the once-over before introducing himself as the landlady's son-in-law, then demanded to know why d had pretended not to be at home when they clearly were. What with several months' rent being past due and there being no answer at the door, he'd thought the place was empty. d waited for the man to offer some rice cake. And Kim Gwija's persimmon punch. The man offered neither, and instead told d through the window that Kim Gwija had been taken into hospice care. He did not say that she would now progress towards death, free from pain, immersed in a comfortable dream state for the remainder of her days thanks to legal injections of substantial quantities of

30   dd's Umbrella

morphine, but d understood this to be the case from the routine, indifferent look in the man's eyes. d was about to speak when Kim Gwija's son-in-law placed his hands on his knees and heaved himself up. He asked what had happened to the room and, when d didn't answer, if this room had always been like this.

Always?

I mean, was it originally in this state.

d stared up at the men's feet before saying, Yes, it really is as you say, this room was always like this.

The first thing d heard upon opening their door was the sound of a motor. It was midafternoon on a summer's day. A heat warning had been issued earlier and the outdoor air conditioner unit was churning away, whirring and whining, heating up the air even more. d made their way out of the alley on foot. Their nose was parched, their clothes felt much too loose and were in fact too loose, but their feet were cool and their steps light. d strode down the sunny side of the street. The street was hot, which pleased d, as the general heat absorbed the specific warmth of objects. With each step their clothes flapped and wound about their belly, thighs, calves, and around their shoes, but the warmth of the fabric and leather was almost unnoticeable in the hot air. Summers are fantastic, d thought, I wish more things would melt into air, how great it would be if the world was always this warm. They walked down the sun-filled streets in their winter clothes: a pullover worn day in and day out for, d had lost count of how many days, and a pair of crumpled cotton trousers. d's gaunt cheeks were covered in a sparse growth, their chest sported the dried trail of vomit from several nights ago. Their hair, armpits, and groin hadn't been washed in a while and people wrinkled their noses as they passed by and caught a whiff. d was unconcerned. Their eyes sparkled and they carried their head high as if out in daylight for the first time. d felt something very close to happiness. They forged ahead, fully aware of the momentousness of all this being upright and walking. Their legs felt feather-light, their joints moved in a buoyant and effortless manner like lean, well-oiled parts. Eventually however, confusion set in. The pace was much too quick and it seemed their senses couldn't keep up. Despite continuing in a straight line there was a feeling of circling in place, as if they were inside some rapidly turning slide projector... Street scenes sloshed about, borne away and back again on a jumbled tide of colours, none of it observable. d's feet and knees began to stiffen and when the pain became unbearable, d stopped. Simply came to a standstill and remained there, unmoving, overcome with fatigue and too exhausted to care where they were or how far they'd managed to get. The 6623 bus was pulling out of a stop, sputtering fumes. d saw a round coin stuck fast to the ground as if it had been crushed by traffic.

Staring down at the flat coin, d thought about how the outside didn't feel much like the outside. They had opened their door and ventured out into the world, alone, after a long time spent holed up inside, but the outdoors still felt a lot like the indoors, as if d had merely moved from one small pocket into another barely larger small pocket. The air was surprisingly familiar and stale. *And yes... it really is as you say, this room was always like this.*

d had thought they'd lost something, had believed their world had changed for good. But this turned out to be untrue. It occurred to them now that they'd simply reverted to the

32 dd's Umbrella

past, to how things had always been. dd had been the exception: dd's existence in the world, in d's world, had been the exception. I haven't changed, I've simply returned to my usual self. d closed their mouth. A cold, burning sensation pierced their ears, like a spear thrust in one side and out the other. d felt the vestiges of intervening time return from their long, circuitous trajectory. The world teemed with noise.

3

d settled the back rent with Kim Gwija's son-in-law and left flat B02. They found a new place at 580 Banghwadong in Gangseogu and paid six months' rent up front. The room came with a bed and a desk but without windows or a security deposit, and rent was ₩380,000 per month. The wallpaper, desk, blanket, and pillow were inherited, unwiped and unwashed, from the previous tenant. The pillow was damp and stained, the blanket had strands of grey hair stuck to it, and the desk corners were littered with crumbs. This was room 15 of Samsung Gosiwon. The room opposite was identical in size and layout, and along the narrow corridor stretched a dozen of these units, the corridor itself branching into several corners like a maze. The oiled-paper floor was sticky with dust, the shoe cabinet by the doorway was as large as the ones in public bathhouses and always full. Opposite the mirror, stuck to the wall by the exit, was a fire extinguisher chained to the wall and a coin telephone. The latter wouldn't have looked out of place in an antique curio shop, but it was a working phone and not merely decoration.

The phone wouldn't take prepaid phone cards, it only accepted ₩10, ₩50, and ₩100 coins and of course went through them at an amazing rate, so you had to have a fistful of

34   dd's Umbrella

coins at the ready. d's room was close enough to the phone that they could hear most of what was said, usually in Chinese or in Korean: I've sent some money, please wire some more; How is so-and-so's health, I'm not doing so well myself; I miss you, I'll kill you. d lay or sat on their mattress listening to the hum of shared space — coins dropping, feet dragging, doors shutting, someone sighing, blowing their nose, sneezing, swearing, slurping noodles. So many people packed in like sardines, yet hardly exchanging a word of greeting even when they passed each other in the corridor. The silence amplified each sound and movement made behind the walls. d slept badly.

d's lengthy and unauthorised absence from work had cost them their job, but they found work collecting and loading parcels at Sewoon Market in Jangsadong, Jongno. The workday started around noon, but d left the gosiwon early each morning. After stopping at a convenience store to pick up a ready meal, disposable chopsticks, and a water, they'd walk to the local community centre where they could sit with a view of the indoor swimming pool. d took their time over the usual rice topped with potatoes and carrots simmered in bulgogi sauce, gazing at the swimmers below. Every morning, from seven to half-past seven. The swimming pool extended over three stories of the building and was the heart of the community centre. The pool itself was at basement level and sparkled all day with the light pouring in through south-facing windows so tall and wide they formed a glass wall. Eight lanes were visible from where d sat. d followed with their eyes as people advanced through the lanes in butterfly stroke, heads and arms rising quietly out of and gliding back under the water. New arrivals waded in with backs hunched. Swimmers emerging from the pool wiped wet lips with wet hands. The taste: salty lukewarm water mixed with a chlorine-based disinfectant — d knew it too. Monday, Tuesday, Wednesday, Thursday, Friday: every day people came to swim and every day d heard the lifeguard's whistle break through the viewing window. The scenes unfolding beyond the transparent wall glided off d like water down impermeable glass. For d the place offered something to look at while they ate and drank, but their mind remained blank, disengaged. None of it made an impression or elicited a reaction. If that clear, clean space were to fold in half, it would be of no consequence to them. d chewed and swallowed, a mechanical action of the jaw and gullet that ended with a glob lodged in the pit of their stomach.

We saw it together, d reminded themself. The charred spot left by the lightning. That's what dd said, but I have no memory of us being there together. d thought back to when they had first heard about this, how they had asked, Really? and been surprised by dd's answer. d had gone over the scene in the classroom many times, each time finding it strange that dd was entirely absent from it. But by now d was inclined to think that they did remember a similar situation, that they had indeed been talking to someone else crouched alongside them. That the two of them had looked at the mark together... Yes, that was the memory. Even if who that someone was remained unclear. d began to imagine that they had smelled something sour and sweaty, not unlike the odour of glue or adhesive. Yes — by now this was definitely a memory d possessed.

Occasionally they even dreamt about it. In the dream d was an adult gazing down on their younger self and a young dd as they crouched over the classroom floor, their small backs intent and focused. dd looked so small, small enough to be scooped up

36 dd's Umbrella

in d's grown-up arms, that d was convinced they could reach out and keep dd safe. I can save dd, d would think in the dream, only to realise they had no arms. Upon waking, d would have to watch as the world rushed in at full volume and swept the two young children away in its seething current, feeling entirely mute and powerless. The dream ended with a thunderous scream, and reality yawned once more in stunned silence.

Every day on their way to work, d passed a billboard. There it loomed, each day: the blown-up image of an actor in a cosmetics ad, the brown spot on the tip of their nose powdered to appear less prominent. The sight of it reminded d of the spot on dd's hand. dd had liked to keep their hands well manicured but loathed hangnails and used to tear or bite them off. One time, they'd drawn blood right above the nail of their right ring finger. The wound left a dark reddish-brown mark. Blood had pooled under the skin and, instead of being reabsorbed, had hardened there to form a small spot. A reddish-brown spot resembling a drop of water. A wound as small as that had been big enough to leave a scar, whereas dd's death... dd's death hasn't left the tiniest trace on me, d thought. Life has refused to grant me even that.

d usually took the 602 bus to work. One day, the driver was swerving dizzily between lanes, causing passengers to sway and jolt with each turn of the wheel. As the bus slowed to approach the next stop, d leaned towards the driver's seat and told them to drive properly. What was that? I said drive properly, like a proper driver. What did you just say to me? Fucking drive properly, shithead. You better move back, the driver said, passengers can't cross this line, it's dangerous, move back, will you. The nerve, d thought with contempt, incensed by the driver's refusal to acknowledge their words. Turning round to head back to their seat, d saw the other passengers staring with guarded contempt not at the driver but at them, and seeing the doors standing open, they stepped off the bus. They found themself at a causeway somewhere between two bodies of water, Hangang and Anyangcheon. Hardly anyone got on or off at this stop, apart from the occasional weekend picnickers. The bus clanged as if shaking off a nuisance and trundled on without d. Shaking with rage, d followed the bus on foot, ranting at the air around them. Eventually they grew quiet. The breeze off the river dried their face. Disillusion, contempt: these were possible. Why wouldn't they be? After that day, d occasionally crossed the river on foot. They nursed what emotions were available to them.

At Sewoon Market, countless objects passed d's hands. It was a world of cigarette-smoking men, stagnant puddles, and all manner of goods. Apart from the tradespeople, next to no one sought out the market, and what with the numerous empty shops, the place seemed to be careening towards permanent closure. But at night, in the ground floor car park, which served as the depot, parcels would pile up in colossal heaps. d's task was to collect, sort, and load these onto courier trucks. From lunchtime on, d visited each place of business with a big wad of shipping labels and asked if they had anything to send. If the answer was no, d moved on to the next shop; if yes, d would affix a label on the boxed parcel, hand over the original to the seller, and carry the parcel down to the ground floor. Everything they touched held the cloying warmth, but d was far too busy and the work far too strenuous for them to pay much notice. There was only one lift servicing the entire building and the building caretakers actively discouraged

38   dd's Umbrella

couriers and delivery workers from using it. d spent a lot of time arguing with or being sworn at by the caretakers on their endless traipses up and down the eight floors. d was responsible for all of the parcels leaving Sewoon Market and the parts shops in the surrounding alleys. From sorting, which had to be done outside official working hours, to the loading of the final parcel, each day involved over ten hours of intense labour. By the end of the day d would be famished and would grab a bowl of noodles in Jongno before returning to room 15, as empty-handed as when they had left it in the morning. After a short night, they'd set off again early to breakfast then head straight to work. d kept to themself and didn't talk much with anyone. They consigned nothing to memory and clocked off each day with sleep. This became d's daily routine.

One evening, d was scanning the labels and loading parcels in the depot when they felt a nudge in their back and heard someone say: You know me, right?

4

Yeo Sonyeo was born in 1946 as the eldest son of eight siblings. He had two older sisters and five younger siblings. Their father Yeo Joong-geon died of lung cancer the year the youngest was born, after which their mother No Jae-soon began providing room and board to a circus troupe for extra money, discovered an unexpected talent, and went on to raise all eight children by selling bowls of sujebi. Their house was in the area that in the old days had been called Nureori, then Songjeongli under Japanese occupation, and finally Gonghangdong for its proximity to the airport.

Yeo Sonyeo learned to take a beating from both classmates and seniors who teased and bullied him throughout his childhood for his girlish name, a name that literally meant *girl*. Stocky and compact with a short neck and a strong head and grip, Yeo Sonyeo considered his teeth his best physical attribute. He swore he could pluck nails out of metal pipes with his teeth, which he proceeded to demonstrate both when others were present and when they were not, sometimes out of a desire to boast and at other times out of boredom, or simply because he could not be bothered to fetch a claw hammer.

He learned his craft at an electronics high school and was hired as an apprentice by a shop in Gonghangdong. With his

40   dd's Umbrella

sharp eye and deft hand, he was good at fixing things, and
when his apprenticeship was over, he was able to open a small
repair shop in the Cheonggyecheon area with the help of his
sisters. Radios, TVs, fans, audio systems... He accepted any
and all electronic goods, but after burning his arm one winter
while repairing a microwave, he narrowed his range to
loudspeakers and amps. The construction of Sewoon Market's
two buildings, Ga and Na, were completed in 1967, and that
was the year Yeo Sonyeo opened his shop. He remembered the
opening ceremony for the commercial section of Sewoon
Market. Park Chung-hee and Yuk Young-soo, accompanied by
a young Park Ji-man prettily dressed up in Western clothes,
visited the Western clothing shop on the second floor, and
while the first family looked through the selection of boys'
trousers, Yeo Sonyeo, though unable to witness that particular
scene, had nonetheless stood among the crowd thronging the
building and looked up at this dream of an edifice, taking in its
precipitous height. Building Ga of Sewoon Market, the one
Yeo Sonyeo was craning to stare at, consisted of retail space up
to the fourth floor and residential apartments with an adjoining
main atrium from the fifth floor up. Kitchens decorated with
tiles, individual hot-water supplies, beds that could be folded
down from the wall: the Republic of Korea's first New Style
departmansion. Yeo Sonyeo watched as the commercial market
thrived even as the residential space quickly went out of
fashion, then, in the late 1970s, once the residents had vacated
the apartments due to the lack of parking space and the
delinquent surroundings, he burrowed his way into the fifth
floor. There he remained for thirty-six years.

After the 1990s, as commerce declined and customers and
vendors alike got fewer and fewer, shops emptied on the lower

floors and became more affordable; regardless, Yeo Sonyeo remained on the fifth floor, especially as access to the fourth floor down to the first was limited at night, for the fire doors were padlocked after midnight. He needed the doors to always be open since he started the day late and worked into the early hours. Yeo Sonyeo remained for ten years in no. 564 before moving to no. 568, then returned, several years later, to no. 564. The window that had let rain in even when it was shut, the hole in the ceiling through which rat droppings used to fall had been neatly done up in the meantime. There was an awning over the window now and a fresh coat of paint on the walls. Yeo Sonyeo was content, and he filled the space with old amps and got to work repairing them, bowing his head once more under the naked bulb light as he had done for so many years.

But recently he had been asked a question.

Where have they all gone? His daughter had asked. I mean, there used to be a lot of people at Sewoon Market. People you knew personally. People who ran their shops for as long as you've run yours. The grown-ups who used to buy me ice cream or crisps or sweets when I dropped by with Ma. Hardly any of them are left now, but where have they all gone?

Where have they gone? Yeo Sonyeo repeated in surprise. Well now… They've gone, haven't they. They all left.

Gone where though?

Some have gone elsewhere, others have passed on.

Yeo Sonyeo had replied indifferently, not wanting to dwell on the subject, and his daughter hadn't pressed him. But later he found himself mulling over her question. Seated at his worktable with a screwdriver in hand, he cast his mind back.

42   dd's Umbrella

Yeo Sonyeo had moved from Gonghangdong to Banghwadong, and from Banghwa back to Gonghang over the years, never venturing outside the district of Gangseo but always criss-crossing from west to north and north to west in the same overlapping lines. Apart from his family, most of the people he'd come across in life were at Sewoon, and of the people who he had gotten to know at the market there weren't many left, a fact Yeo Sonyeo was only now belatedly contemplating. Mr. Yu of Yumyungsa who did video work, Mr. Baek the audio guy, Mr. Lee the transformer guy, Mr. Kim the cable man, and auntie Kim Eunsong from the corner shop, Eunsong Super, on the fifth floor: these were the ones who, like himself, had remained. But Ms. Kim Eunsong was preparing to hand over her shop and leave, for the fifth floor rarely saw customers these days. Just last week she had visited his shop with her ledger to show him the very first record of his custom at her shop: a day in 1996, when he had purchased one cup ramyeon, one bottle of the energy drink Bacchus, and a pack of This cigarettes. Ms. Kim Eunsong and Yeo Sonyeo had gone over the ledger together, page by page, tallying up the credit still due, and then Yeo Sonyeo had paid her the ₩87,800 in cash and settled his outstanding credit. The ₩800, which Ms. Kim Eunsong had kindly deducted, was still on Yeo Sonyeo's worktable.

Only a few years ago, all he'd had to do was step outside his shop to have places to go and people to visit within walking distance. He hadn't even bothered with hello, he used to just walk in and ask for the thing, and they'd know exactly which thing and hand it over, the bastards — they were all bastards and swindlers in a way, real crooks the lot of them, though they weren't such a bad lot either all told... Will I ever see them

Hwang 43

again maybe in the next life, those pesky buggers who used to drive me mad until I got used to them? The audio sellers, parts sellers, transformer technicians, loudspeaker manufacturers, the older folk who could knock off counterfeit brand labels that looked like the real thing, the bevy of other technicians. Every one of them had lived through an era, together, here. Where did they all go? Each time this question resurfaced, Yeo Sonyeo was confronted with their absence, his remaining presence, and his own impending absence all at once. It was that kind of question. Yeo Sonyeo felt a sudden, awkward loneliness. He'd been peering inside broken machines forever, and only now, looking up at long last, did he realise his repair shop had washed up in some remote corner of the world, on the border of an unpeopled wilderness.

Yeo Sonyeo leaned back in his chair, gingerly feeling out an aching back tooth with his tongue. The chair creaked, tipped back. Inside the oscilloscope the thin green wave was flowing levelly, waiting for a stimulus, and on the worktable where disorder signalled order, a Maranz 2325 he'd opened up earlier lay bearing its dusty innards. The iron for pressing lead lay on a metal plate scorched by cigarettes. Coins, screws, springs, black and silver metal shavings, IC chips and the like were scattered or piled variously as though someone had grabbed a fistful and sprinkled them willy-nilly. Yeo Sonyeo no longer used his teeth to remove nails. He didn't dare. What he'd once considered his sturdiest asset had been deteriorating over several years now. The first horizontal blueish line on his front tooth had appeared eight years ago, a fissure that had finally become apparent as the rot took hold. And it wasn't the only one. His front teeth went on rotting along that minute crack until they fell out leaving only the roots, and several of his back teeth

44   dd's Umbrella

came apart in his mouth like chunks of plaster while he was eating. He had three implants fitted to replace the molars. These weren't sufficient, but he barely had bone left under his gums so three were all they were able to screw in. The dentist had mentioned filling in the gums with some hard foam-like substance onto which they could screw in the implants, but Yeo Sonyeo had misgivings in addition to finding the cost onerous and had grumbled and refused. The consequence being that he now had to muddle by as best he could with the few feeble teeth he had left next to the three implants. He couldn't chew as he once had and lost interest in eating. Removable dentures would have helped, only Yeo Sonyeo hated dentures and would refuse them to his death.

Yeo Sonyeo switched off the lamp illuminating the Maranz. Locking his fingers, he nestled his hands on his belly and said to himself, right, let's have a think about this, have a proper think now, because they haven't all gone have they, no, they haven't, not exactly. Some got a break and skedaddled out of here good and early, now they drive their cars to the golf course every weekend. As for the rest... *I'm* the rest. I'm what's left. I still know every nook and cranny of this building like I know the back of my hand, but in this entire place there's not even ten left who know me. What is it they say of a situation like this... ? Yeo Sonyeo scrunched his face to quell the rising despair, stood up and began to pace back and forth in the narrow passage, then stopped suddenly and stooped over the parcels he'd received over the two previous days. He peered at the labels: a Fisher 250 that Kang Hayeon had sent all the way from Jeonju, an Altec monoblock sent along from Kim's Audio up in Seongbukgu... There was a fairly small box as well, but after glancing at the label Yeo Sonyeo realised it had been delivered to him by mistake. It was addressed for Daerim Market, which was on the other side of Cheonggyecheon. The box was heavy for its size, he reckoned it must be a transformer. Yeo Sonyeo flipped the parcel over a few times as if handling a large die, then headed out of the shop with it.

Eight o'clock on a winter evening like any other. Yeo Sonyeo walked downstairs, away from the landing where the porters left their back carriers at the end of each day. Sleet had been falling as the sun set, and the stairs and floors were covered in sludge and footprints. It was near closing time. His breath steamed up white. Yeo Sonyeo regretted not having thought to put on his jacket as he headed for the first floor. The rumble of engines as delivery vans pulled in echoed thunderously against the ceiling of the car park. This ceiling was also the bottom of the third-floor walk deck and black with exhaust fumes.

Cigarette butts and peeled-off backing paper were littered around a mountain of boxes. Every parcel due to leave the market that night was first collected here. From closing time on, the car park became the loading station. Kyoungdong, Logen, Yellow, Hyundai, KGB, and other smaller carriers used the car park as a depot for sorting and loading. Usually the managers overseeing the shipping labels kept an eye on the parcels while their coworkers went from shop to shop for pick-ups. Once evening fell, the larger delivery companies opened up a long crate-like container for their cargo. Inside there was just enough room for one person to sit behind a desk installed with a printer. Here a gruff woman with prominent cheekbones sat calculating fees and handing out the labels. The goods started trickling in from noon, and by evening would form several heaps. It was the same every day. Yeo Sonyeo

46 dd's Umbrella

walked past the Kyoungdong Express loading area and headed north, in the direction of Jongmyo, thinking again how curious all this was. How could so much freight accumulate in this near-empty market? Hardly anyone came and went here. Who was buying all these products? Ghosts?

The commercial zone of Sewoon Market had changed, that was irrefutable, and it was clearly headed towards decline. Walking past the shuttered fronts of the audio shops, Yeo Sonyeo thought these businesses must have borne the brunt of the downturn. Before, people would browse or simply wander about the shops or come specifically to listen to this or that audio system. Those who came to have a listen would likely return, and after a few visits would eventually make a purchase. A sale, simply from people walking past. This was impossible now; passersby had become that rare. Online sales, sure: people bought lamps, cables, electric heaters, electric pads, electric fans, brooms, sockets, all sorts of everyday items off the web. Hence the mountain of products that amassed every night at the loading station. But to Yeo Sonyeo the people who bought these were as good as ghosts. They had no footfall, they had no face.

The market had become a warehouse.

Those who were able to adapt remained, those who couldn't left. Yeo Sonyeo had remained thus far, but undoubtedly belonged to the latter category. Business was brisk yet visitors were few and far between, and shops stood increasingly empty. The strangeness of it all, he thought. The place has become a warehouse stocked only with goods that sell, with only a handful of supervisors left to manage it. In time one vast warehouse and a single supervisor might be all that remains. It was a desolate image. Yeo Sonyeo pursed his lips. He felt the skin of his neck crawl and chills run up and down his body, but he wasn't sure if this was because of the absurd image or the cold. A delivery car backed up in his direction, honking its horn. Cursing, Yeo Sonyeo jumped over the puddle of piss-coloured water. He headed to the Logen section. Loading was in full swing. Not a single person wore a jacket; everyone transporting boxes were in sweat-soaked shirts and wore scarves or masks over their mouth and chin. Yeo Sonyeo spotted the courier who stopped by his shop every day and walked over towards their steaming back. Hey, you, he said. You know me, right?

5

This man's standing way too close to me, thought d. Square head, hunched shoulders, scrunched-up face, brows of different lengths peppered with grey, the stink of tobacco — d didn't know what to make of this unexpected intrusion. Was the man angry? His forehead was blue from the cold and furrowed, his black eyes stared, his voice was low and cantankerous. It was difficult to understand what he was saying. The man extended a hand and thrust something at d, then turned and walked away. d stared at the receding man's back, at his reddish gingham shirt and faded brown vest. The box they'd accepted out of reflex was heavy. It weighed down their left arm. d remained rooted to the spot, dazed by the encounter, then frowned: they could feel the abrupt impression made on their back by the man's nudging finger. It had left an itching sensation.

Do I know you? No. d didn't know the man in the slightest.

You know me, right?

This was all d could make out of the man's muttering. His words were closer to text than speech, an utterance not so much heard as seen.

50   dd's Umbrella

d resumed their work but kept thinking about the man's question. The brief exchange replayed on their mind all night. For something unexpected had occurred. The man was not known to d, yet d knew him. Hadn't known him from Adam when the man prodded them, but as soon as he asked if d knew him, d had felt at a loss for words. Because they did know. I don't know you, why would I? d had wanted to retort, only to realise on hearing the question and glancing at the man that this was in fact a familiar face. d knew the man.

How though?

d knew the way to the man's shop. Take the lift on the Cheonggyecheon side of the building to the fifth floor then cross the hall in the direction of Jongno; or, take the stairs up from the Jongno side and turn right at the fifth floor atrium with its high skylight before stepping into the gloomy doorway of no. 564. Of the three rooms there, the middle one was the man's shop. d could find it in no time, even with their eyes closed. They'd been visiting that room twice a day for the last seven months after all.

And now d was, once again, passing by Kim Jeongyeop's shop with a handful of shipping labels. There was a whiff of sweat. Under the stairs that connected the third-floor walk deck to the car park on the Jongno side of the building, at the corner of Clock Alley, was where Kim Jeongyeop's cable shop stood. Long and short, thick and thin, electrical cables hung in bundles inside the tiny shop where Kim Jeongyeop lifted dumbbells all day long, his stereo set to a classical music station. He wore sleeveless shirts that revealed his arm muscles and lifted weights every chance he got until he broke a sweat. He had a decent stereo system, the sound was smooth and weighty, and with it he'd transformed the long car park stretching north to south from Jongno to Cheonggyecheon into a corridor of music filled with Bach and Dvořák. Kim Jeongyeop turned his stereo off before lowering his shutters, usually at seven o'clock in the evening. When the music stopped, d knew the vans would start pulling up. d walked into Clock Alley. The dark, narrow passage had never been repaired properly, it dipped in the middle from the unfathomed comings and goings of people ferrying all manner of goods over the decades. The concrete drain cover that dated back to the 1970s was greened with moss.

d went past a few glass displays carrying old wristwatches and faded watch straps and stopped by the lightbulb shop Geumhosa. A man with white hair sat attaching feet onto a bulb, and raised his head when d entered. d knew the man's name was Yoon Choong-gil. This older man spent the whole day seated at his table, which sat askew by the doorway, extending the lead-in wires or, as he called them, the *feet* of his little bulbs. He might attach feet where there were none, as he'd been asked to, or extend those that were too short. Until fairly recently he'd done all this himself, but d had stopped by one day to pick up a parcel and discovered that Yoon Choong-gil had hired an assistant in the meantime, a man who appeared to be as elderly and grey-haired as himself. Now two equally elderly men sat working at Geumhosa, the goods for d waiting in a neat stack by their feet.

d loaded the boxes from Geumhosa into their handcart and as usual headed back to the loading station by way of Myeong-in Retail. This parts shop stood out for being perhaps the only establishment that saw a brisk trade amid businesses about to close down or that had already folded. Its proprietor was a woman of middle age with impeccable posture and lips that

52 dd's Umbrella

were always curled into a sneer. She sold electronic components, transistors, and IC chips, and was the best person to consult about replacement parts for discontinued components. d knew that the woman's name was Kang Sookjin and that she had a habit of writing the final consonant of her first name, ㄴ, the one that sounded like n, with a heavier hand relative to the rest of her name. Now she was packing parts from the glass display into several small zipper bags and answering a call over speakerphone. *Got any TIP40s laying around?* What do you think? *What's with the attitude?* Look who's talking! She jabbed a button to end the call and opened her eyes wide at d as if to say, What an ass, eh?

d ran into the shoe shop lady at Baek San Audio. She was haggling with Baek San, the owner of the shop, over his shoes. Look at your shoes, chief, your shoes are all dirty, she was saying, sure looks like they could do with a clean, and when Baek San said, Didn't you clean them just last week? she retorted with, You mean it's been one whole week? Do you brush your teeth once a week, hmm? No, you brush them every day, so why would you clean your shoes just the once? The woman had a basket full of slippers in her cart, and she'd take people's shoes and hand them a pair of slippers. There were already several pairs of shoes as well as the worn and tattered slippers, each neatly arranged and poking out of the basket. d didn't know the name of this woman, as she never sent or received her ware by courier, but did know her face and the location of the shoe repair shop where she took the collected shoes to be cleaned. There were no boxes for d today at Baek San Audio, so d headed on to the next shop: the next stop on their daily route, a place that was familiar and filled with known faces and voices. If any one of these people were to nudge me and demand if I knew them, it wouldn't do to say no and besides how could I, d thought, when these are the folk I see day in and day out, in their various worn-down, squalid, strange, and distinct spaces.

On the stairs that led up from lightings to home appliances, d found themself blocked by a porter, or their carrier. The jige was packed with two loudspeakers and a carton box and gently swayed from side to side as it slowly rose up the steps. d had to follow its gradual ascent as there wasn't enough room to squeeze past. The load on the jige looked as high and as heavy as a hill. It was probably the porter's last delivery for the day. From behind d could make out neither the porter's face nor their upper body, but their feet and calves were visible beneath the contraption, straining with care as they trod each step. The porter was bent at the waist at an angle that was nearly parallel to the incline. Once the goods had been delivered, the porter would return to the landing on the fifth floor of Building Ga and open the padlocked crate that had been assigned to them. d knew that the porters kept their bags and clothes in those crates. And that they dressed and undressed next to them without so much as a screen to hide behind. It was a sight d came across every day: porters baring their backs and legs, turned ruddy with labour, to change out of their work clothes, after which they'd park their jiges next to the crates and retire for the day. d had also observed how the porters faced forward when climbing up the stairs with their loads but made their way down backs first to prevent serious injury from a fall. How they would carry things out to the car park for ₩5,000 tips.

And so on, each day.

54   dd's Umbrella

d knew them all.

So? So what? d pulled their cap lower and scowled. You want to know if I know you? If the same thing were to happen in a place other than here, if someone were to prod them in the back and ask such a thing, d would never recognise them, would answer no, because no, they wouldn't know. Because there wouldn't be a reason not to know them nor indeed to know them. They'd be no different from the many other people d despised. They'd be just as repugnant as the people who eat with their tongues hanging out, who blatantly stare, who instead of apologising gawk at you, who bump into you, who jab you with whatever they happen to be carrying and don't even realise, being that obtuse or, if they do realise, are uncaring, people who thrust their muddled personality comprised of an inflated sense of ego and meagre self-esteem in your face. Not the least bit different from all those strangers. The people who lie their way through life.

d sat on the steps that led up to the deck, removing their gloves to cool the heat of all the objects they'd touched. The sun was setting. Classical music still flowed from Kim Jeongyeop's stereo. The neutral voice of an opera singer, not marked by gender, singing a tune d recognised even if they didn't know the title. There was a visible crack running horizontally along the railing. It was long and wide enough for d to make out a distant shop sign. One blow of the hammer or a few kicks of the foot, and the whole railing might come away. d had heard the market folk discussing the sheer solidity of this building. Bash it with a hammer and you'd barely leave a dent even as your hammer was ruined, they said. That's because the bastards who designed this place studied architecture in Japan, and they threw all the best available

Hwang   55

technology and material at it, so no wonder it's this solid. Back in the 1990s there were attempts to have it demolished, but they ran the numbers and it turned out the cost of letting the building stand was cheaper by far, that's how solid it was. But d had noticed several cracks in their daily trek up and down the building. These stairs for instance — from the battered look of them, d wouldn't be surprised if they washed away in the heavy rains this summer, leaving only the skeletal steel frame. d put their gloves back on and went up the remaining steps.

This building will never fall.

Though many people made this claim, d had yet to come across anyone actively taking measures to maintain the building or guard against disrepair. People here only *said* it was indestructible. They uttered these words of faith lightly, as though theirs was a fickle and careless faith. But here were the cracks, plain as day. Flawless and flawed were but two sides of a coin — sooner or later they would be reversed. And faith would be turned inside out and what spilled forth would smear every face...

d stepped into no. 564, labels in hand. The felt covering on the floor caught under their soles. There was a smell of ammonia and solder. Machines with jagged edges were piled high like stalagmites. The man who had intruded on d the day before was seated behind the desk. He wore the same red gingham shirt and faded brown vest. Two small drivers were poking out from the vest's front pocket. He had the sort of build that made him appear larger when seated than when he was standing. He was looking inside an amplifier under the light of a gooseneck lamp. He seemed snug behind his table, and so relaxed he appeared almost deflated.

56   dd's Umbrella

When d didn't move from their spot, the man raised his head and looked at d.

Do *you* know *me*?

The man looked at d, chewing at something in his mouth, before replying: I do.

How?

Seen you.

When?

Uh, every day?

Do you know my name though?

What is it you want?

I want to know if you know my name.

Yeo Sonyeo put a hand in his vest pocket and fumbled with the drivers as he considered d. He remembered d's predecessor. Somewhat older than the usual delivery workers, that man had been a friendly, cheeky sort. He'd made the rounds with the new hire, and that's when Yeo Sonyeo first saw d. Kid here's taking over my beat, he'd announced. The novice standing a step behind. To do what exactly, Yeo Sonyeo had thought at the sight of the sickly youth. Hair and face dull and lifeless, joints sharp without a hint of fat. Who knew what they'd been up to or where they'd been; there was even a large, blunt scar on their chin. The kid didn't say much and had no manners, Yeo Sonyeo concluded. Even at their predecessor's urging, the kid barely managed a head dip. This one will never stick, Yeo Sonyeo had thought with exasperation. He remembered not only d's predecessor but the one before, and the one before that as well. Every single one of them lively, raring to go. But in time even the healthiest and brightest turned gloomy and reserved. Unable to bear the work, the unrelenting intensity of it, most quit after a couple of days, a week, a few months at best. This new arrival would be no different. Yeo Sonyeo expected they wouldn't last much longer than the other youths who'd flitted by. But d managed to muddle through the first and second weeks, then through all of autumn, and here they were now in winter. Each day of each week, d had shown up without fail. Over those weeks Yeo Sonyeo had noticed d's appearance change: the pallor darkening, the posture straightening from wilted to sinewy, their movements becoming increasingly agile with the nimbleness of muscles not superficially built up but strengthened through daily use. The vague stare became focused, and pretty soon they were handling heavier loads and assigned a larger beat.

Recently, in Jongno, Yeo Sonyeo had caught sight of d on their delivery bike. The perennial cap gone, the longish black hair swept back to reveal the face that so often remained covered, chin jutted to feel the wind on their face. They'd looked at ease in the saddle of the motorbike, and reaching the corner of Jongno-2-ga, they'd swerved the bike towards Cheonggyecheon and disappeared. Yeo Sonyeo had laughed, without knowing why. Since that day, he'd paid more attention to d. The kid didn't speak if they could help it and was gruff to the point of rudeness — that much hadn't changed. They barely greeted you despite the daily drop-ins, let alone laughed at your jokes. Standing close enough that with a slip their foreheads could easily have bumped together, they'd fill in the shipping label in silence and without so much as a glance at you. But there was an unvarying consistency in all this that, in the end, Yeo Sonyeo had to accept that this was simply what the kid was and always had been like.

58   dd's Umbrella

And now here was that same kid walking into his shop, eyes all ablaze and staring, to demand if Yeo Sonyeo knew their name. What's this? What have I done to deserve such cheek from you? Yeo Sonyeo looked at d in bewilderment. When have I seen you? Why, every day, every single fucking day, he was about to retort, when d's face abruptly changed colour — the blood drained right out of it, as though in fright or shock. They lowered their head. The defiant energy vanished, leaving confusion and uncertainty. d stood there, unspeaking, rumpling the cap and the wad of shipping labels in their hands and staring at the floor; then, hastily donning their cap, they made to leave.

Here. Yeo Sonyeo gestured to the JBL loudspeaker he used as a table. Have a bite before you go.

A warped aluminium tray sat atop the thigh-high speaker, holding the bowl of jajangmyeon that had been delivered moments before d showed up. Yeo Sonyeo lifted the receiver and dialled the number for Donghaeru. Another jajang, he ordered. He turned back to resume his work: a turntable a Kim somebody from Yeosu had left in his care a fortnight ago. Yeo Sonyeo had fixed the wavering pitch and the issue with the tonearm slinking back to the cradle; it was time to test it out. He grabbed an album from the haphazardly shelved vinyl between the desk and the wall, placed it on the turntable, and adjusted the stylus. There was a brief sound like the crunching of sand, followed by the dragging first notes of an Elvis Presley song. d brought over a chair and sat in front of the bowl of black bean noodles. They removed their cap, placed it on an amp, then sat blankly, before pulling the bowl closer. Yeo Sonyeo pressed the Stop button, then the Start button. The tonearm returned at a stable angle to the cradle then glided back to the platter. Yeo Sonyeo pushed the Lift button to suspend the stylus and find the right spot, then pressed Lift again. The stylus settled slowly on the first track. The music resumed.

Yi Chulhee, the proprietor of Donghaeru and Yeo Sonyeo's pool hall partner, came by to personally deliver the second bowl of noodles. Oh, it's you, he remarked when he saw d. What are *you* doing here, Logen?

6

Can we hear it again? d asked.

They meant the song, 'Love Me Tender'.

Every year at Christmas, d and dd had treated themselves to a lavish dinner, after which they would return home to drink expensive wine and snack on a big cake studded with fruits stewed in syrup and a platter of cheese, buttered bread, smoked salmon, and thinly sliced onions while listening to carols on the radio. As far as d could remember, it must have been on Christmas day the year before last that they heard this song. dd had been lounging after the second bottle of wine, but burst out laughing when the music came on. dd hadn't liked Elvis Presley any more than d had. The name immediately conjured up images of the singer in his white top with the tricolour beading of the Stars and Stripes, the flares that were too tight around his thighs, and the red flower necklace on his bared chest — all of which was a bit ludicrous, and neither of them had much liked how he wailed his songs. dd hugged a cushion and laughed and said, This is why I don't like his music, and to think how often I've had to listen to this particular song whether I wanted to or not, and each time it stops me short and I think, What on earth... how can anyone sing with such tenderness, it's absurd, but each time it also makes me happy. I

62 dd's Umbrella

find it funny, really, funny enough to be sad, but it also makes me weirdly happy... When the needle touched the LP and this song of all songs started playing in Yeo Sonyeo's repair shop, d sat very still and listened. The song wasn't the least bit funny, and it certainly didn't make d happy. It was too famous, too familiar, and much too tender for there to be anything absurd left about it. A song heard a few too many times. The sound, though, was something d hadn't heard before. Bewildered, d threw their head back.

This sound.

To hear that very thing, d took a good look at the turntable and the loudspeakers. Then at Yeo Sonyeo hunched over his worktable, and at the vertical blinds obscuring the grimy windowsill, the clutter covering the walls, the amplifiers stacked on the floor. Every inch of the space and all the objects in it were resonating with the sound emerging from the speakers. d had never heard anything like it, never having owned a turntable or amplifier or loudspeakers. It was a sound that turned space into space. dd would have heard it, though. dd had owned vinyl. d listened intently until the end and asked if they could hear it again. Yeo Sonyeo pressed Stop, waited a beat, then pressed Start. All the while d could hear an irregular yet consistent buzzing noise. d asked what the noise was. That's the sound of the stylus scratching at dust or reading the many defects, the nicks and scratches on the record, Yeo Sonyeo said. The noise was... Yes, it was similar to the zigging in d's ears, the static, but heard together with the music it sounded like... like it was part of the music. d wanted to hear it again, wanted to own it. Where can I get it, d asked.

Get what?

This.

Hwang 63

What do you mean, this?

This thing… the machines that let you hear this type of music.

You mean vintage?

Vintage…

There are plenty downstairs.

Downstairs where?

Take your pick.

But which one.

Have you bought one of these before?

No.

My, my.

How much would it cost to get all this stuff, d asked.

Well, turntable, amplifier… Will you need speakers too? Yeo Sonyeo asked.

d nodded.

In that case, even if you go for what's standard, nothing too fancy or too cheap, it's still going to set you back a good million, Yeo Sonyeo said. You still want one?

I do.

You want me to look into it?

Yes.

Then let's wait a bit, said Yeo Sonyeo. We'll look for the right one.

d said they would wait, then put their cap back on and headed down to the loading station.

It took Yeo Sonyeo a fortnight to assemble a sound system for d: a Dual 731Q turntable, a Fisher 440 amplifier, JBL loudspeakers. It's your first, so no need to be greedy, this is a good start. Yeo Sonyeo was especially pleased with the

64   dd's Umbrella

amplifier: barely a scratch outside, all the buttons nice and intact, the circuitry in clean condition. d would leave the stereo at the shop until the end of their shift, then take it across the river on a delivery bike. The wind was sharp that night. d drove the motorbike slowly and arrived around midnight at the gosiwon. Leaving their bike parked in front of the steps, they moved the amp up to room 15. The loudspeakers were too big to be carried at once, and d had to rest on the way up the stairs and again in the corridor. The caretaker wasn't in his seat. A man in soft rubber slides approached from the other end of the corridor carrying paper cups the size of Baskin-Robbins pints and plastic water bottles and stopped in his tracks when he saw d and the speaker. He seemed surprised but stood aside quietly to let d pass. d heard the man grumble as they squeezed past him but couldn't make out the words nor did they care. d went back for the second speaker, then closed the door of room 15.

From the entrance d looked about to see where best to put the equipment. The speakers, turntable, and amp were piled on the single bed, the mattress sagging under their weight. d had intended to install the stereo between the bed and the wall, but the speakers were bigger than expected. Placing a foot on the mattress to keep the remaining equipment from toppling over, d moved the amp to the floor. With the amp taking up so much space, d would have to strain to step over it in order to reach the desk from the front door. Next, d carefully placed the turntable above the amp. It was bigger than the amp. They'd have to step on the bed as well to get to the desk now. d moved one of the speakers off the bed. It was clear they'd have trouble opening and closing the door if they put both speakers on the floor. d stood next to the bed, not bothering to change out of the work clothes they'd sweated in all day and crossed their arms. They ran a hand through their hair, which was rough from dust and sweat, and looked again at the desk. Above the desk there was a screwed-on shelf; remove that and there might be just enough space on the desk for the speakers and the turntable. d waited outside the empty caretaker's office, then asked to borrow a screwdriver.

What for?

d stood by while the disgruntled caretaker went to look in his toolbox, then returned to their room with the screwdriver. Feeling out the four screws under the shelf with their hand, d loosened them, pressing hard as they turned the screwdriver. The shelf came away from the wall.

The speakers went on either side, the amp in the middle, the turntable on top. Once the transformer — which Yeo Sonyeo had said was a gift, on account of this being d's very first sound system — was positioned, the set was complete. d carefully connected the cables and switched the transformer on. An abrupt sound erupted out of the speakers as a dark orange light lit up the frequency panel of the amp. Room 15 thrummed with the unmistakable flow of electricity. d stepped back and sat on the edge of the bed. There was an engrossed and stubborn manner to the amp and how it seemed to be holding the current close. And there was a smell. Of metal flooded with electricity. Of lead and copper. Of the coil hidden inside the machine heating up, of dust burning... Of blood.

d turned the knob of the input selector to Phono as Yeo Sonyeo had shown him. Now the player was ready. d pressed Start; the small round button disappeared then popped out again with a small click. Like the sound of a small coin being placed on a metal table. The empty turntable rotated and the arm moved towards it. The light of the pale green bulb hidden

66   dd's Umbrella

under the turntable was visible. It was a dim, mean light. There must only be the one tiny bulb. d felt a rush of affection towards that small object, then felt sick to the stomach. It's only a thing. A thing like any other thing. Still d found themself pressing the button. And thinking, I should get dd's vinyl collection back.

That Saturday d paid a visit to Jangmi Mansion. Located at the dead end of a narrow alley, the dark red building had a semi-basement floor and four floors above ground. The waist-high barred gate was half corroded with rust, the metal letters spelling out the name of the building on the wall had turned green, and two of the final consonants had gone missing, leaving JANGMI MA SIO . The building must have been at least thirty years old. dd's parents had recklessly taken out a loan to buy the multiunit, with existing jeonse tenants, and d knew that as recently as a few years ago dd had been struggling to repay part of this loan. dd's room was on the fourth floor, as were the living room and their parents' bedroom, but dd hadn't lived there for long. Mainly because dd's parents, petrified at the size of the place, which was nearly three times as big as their previous flat, had closed off the boiler pipes to each of the rooms in a desperate attempt to save heating money. The first year their family moved into that old building, dd had a cold that lasted through the winter. dd was fond of their parents but the sentiment hadn't been reciprocated much, their parents' attention being entirely focused on the eldest who was sensitive and whose projects never seemed to pan out, and so when it came time to quit expecting anything from them, dd packed a rucksack and a box and left. I thought I'd only take what I couldn't do without, but that turned out not to be a whole lot, dd had told d. They'd looked round the room to see what they could pack in the box, but there hadn't been much that seemed indispensable. Still, wanting to take a few items, if only for the sake of pride, dd had boxed the LPs and the various pens and writing instruments they'd collected over time with their pocket money. And it was that same box that d had come back to claim, the box they had returned to this address after dd's accident.

d pressed the bell and waited outside the metal gate for the door to open, then climbed the stairs to the fourth floor. Gwak Jungeun, dd's older sibling, was waiting on the landing with a stern expression. They wore slides over bare feet and a jersey zipped up to their chin, which was red from the cold. d followed Gwak Jungeun up the metal stairs that led to the roof. They walked past the planter where frozen ornamental cabbage lay scattered like rags and into the oktop room. It was cramped in there, and of the two rooms one was used as the family storage room and the other was occupied by Gwak Jungeun. Gwak Jungeun opened the door of the storage room. Furniture and other knickknacks that were no longer in use were piled inside. As were the boxes d had packed, labelled, and sent on. Some of them hadn't even been opened. d hauled the boxes out and looked through them. In the third box, d found them — dd's old albums, covers disintegrating or stiff with dust: Ella Fitzgerald, Georges Moustaki, Neil Young, Nat King Cole, Patti Page, Sinawi, New Kids on the Block, Shin Haechul, Boney M, Elizaveta Gilels, Vivaldi, Michael Jackson. An erratic collection. Or rather, their musical taste had been interrupted before it had a chance to form.

While d removed the LPs and began stacking them one at a time on the floor, Gwak Jungeun leaned against the door with

68   dd's Umbrella

arms crossed, staring at the back of d's head. Lips pursed in a thin line, hands clenched inside their trouser pockets. d knew the parents had chosen to not be present for this visit. And that Gwak Jungeun was glaring at them as if ready to strike at any moment. Do you want some water, Gwak Jungeun asked in a thick voice. I'm fine, d said without looking back. You're fine? Gwak Jungeun repeated. d said nothing. The floor was ice cold beneath its thin layer of vinyl. The smell from Gwak Jungeun's jersey permeated the entire oktop. Gwak Jungeun wasn't very similar in appearance to dd, but when they slept, when their eyes were closed, then there might be a resemblance, d thought. d's pa and grandpa had shared a likeness by that measure, as d and their parents possibly did too. People who have lived under one roof tend to resemble one another in their most unguarded moments.

The two of us... we didn't get along, Gwak Jungeun had told d. At dd's funeral. It was the middle of the night, they'd come outside for some air. d had never seen Gwak Jungeun speak as much as they spoke that night. It was a full three-day wake. Gwak Jungeun had been sweating profusely. Their black jeogori was wrinkled and wet, had clung to their back. Gwak Jungeun kept digging at the dirt with the toe of their shoe, exposing the grass roots and then trampling the soil back down to cover them again. I didn't pay much attention to them, Gwak Jungeun said.

From when we were kids, we didn't really speak the same language... we didn't play together either. I had nothing to say — well, I didn't have much to say to anyone. I was just a kid from a dirt-poor family. I couldn't be bothered with anything, everything seemed useless and beside the point. As for younger siblings, all I thought about them, if I thought of them at all, was how my life would be better without them, if they didn't exist... I saw the kid on the way home from school once. An eleven-year-old standing outside a fry shop, peering over a messy pile of fried food laid out in the open air. They were carrying a basket in one hand, tongs in the other, agonising over what to get. They looked so earnest, trying to calculate what they could buy with the change they had. My kid sibling. That's what comes back, that's what I keep seeing. That fry shop was run by a mean woman who wouldn't even wash her hands after she'd been to the toilet, and to see my kid sibling take such pains over what she was selling... I had to come out for air, I couldn't stand it inside. I can't bear to look at the photo they have up in there. ₩500 worth of fries. That's all they could afford to put in that damned basket. I'll go mad thinking about it, mad. So. Now you say something. Tell me they were better off towards the end... that they lacked for nothing much, at least in their final months, tell me that, would you?

d ripped the tape off the fourth box. It was crushed from the weight of the other boxes. There wasn't much inside, a few notebooks, some books showing signs of wear, a beginner's German language course book, a bundle of letters tied together with paper string. All of it still warm to the touch. d felt sick again. Unable to continue, they put the stack of LPs into the box, picked it up, and turned around. Gwak Jungeun had disappeared, leaving d alone in the oktop. d stood there with the box for some time before heading down to the fourth floor. Gwak Jungeun was staring at the TV from the sofa. Their chin and nose were red and they had one bare foot propped on a worn brown cushion. d stood and looked at Gwak Jungeun, not knowing how to say goodbye. Going

70 dd's Umbrella

then? Gwak Jungeun asked without lifting their eyes from the TV. Find everything you were looking for? Yeah well... Go on then... And don't even think about coming back... One minute you're dumping everything on us like it's trash, now you're back to collect? Whatever, just get on out of here and... Nah, you know what? Come back... Come back another time, okay?

d placed the LP on the turntable. And closed their eyes at the first hiss of static: the signal that the music was about to begin. The stylus chattered as it traced the groove. Then music filled the room.

The thin surface layer of plywood covering the walls reflected the music completely. d sat facing the speakers, which were covered in a densely woven stretchy fabric and from which a sound emerged that d sensed as a very fine-toothed, delicate comb brushing the crown of their head. Drums, guitars, vocals. The sound was so immense, d could hear nothing else. But the music. The room, being without windows, contained the resonance like a superb soundbox. The creaky bed, the discoloured blanket, the chair holding d's rucksack and jacket, the body sore with muscle pain: each and every thing in the room reverberated with the music, emitting waves that crashed into the walls and echoed around the room. All of it becoming music inside the music.

d dragged the box with the LPs onto the mattress and went through it. Postcards received on school holidays, a handmade Christmas card, diaries with hardback covers. d riffled through a partially used notebook. Even within its few pages dd's handwriting fluctuated. Towards the back, the angular vertical strokes became softer, a little lighter and simpler. dd had liked to collect writing implements, and out of wanting to have something to write down on paper had developed a habit of recording things, from dreams, thoughts, and lines from books to daily outgoings and short anecdotes. d turned the leaves slowly. The sides that were dense with writing seemed stiffer and heavier than the rest. d found an account of a dream on one such page. dd had dreamt that they went to a library and borrowed several books.

The first track of the album was still playing when someone slammed the wall. d found a book with the word REVOLUTION printed across it in block letters at the bottom of the box. d placed the book on their lap. It was a hefty brown book. Hardbound and covered in rough, plain, solid synthetic paper; the title alone printed in black type. The book felt lighter than its bulk suggested and came with two ribbon markers, one yellow and one brown. Someone had marked the first page of the book with a red stamp. It took a while for d to make out the intricate pattern. It was a name, a name d was familiar with: Park Jobae. dd and d's schoolmate. They'd gone to the same primary school. d had heard some time ago that Park Jobae had a cart in the busy shopping district of Myeongdong, that he sold albums from it, but who knew if that was still the case. But what was a book belonging to Park Jobae doing here? d opened the book at random and saw the phrase *the overflow of forces*, and read it back to themself. The overflow. Of forces. An overflow of forces. There was another thump on the wall, this time from the opposite side. d heard someone curse, then hit the wall repeatedly. Now it came from both sides. d pictured the occupants of the neighbouring rooms and smiled. Rooms 14 and 16, identical in layout to room 15 and fitted with the same grimy, if not

72 dd's Umbrella

grimier, bedding and walls, the same cheap furniture made of plywood and contact paper, the same worse-for-wear everyday essentials. I am granting the temporary owners of these rooms and the objects within them the chance to rage, to pound the walls of that one being who is more contemptible and insufferable than themselves or their meagre possessions: their neighbour. Am I enjoying myself? Why yes, yes I am. I am overjoyed. d turned a page of the book. Ah, my neighbours, you who have zero presence and hold no weight except when your bodies hit the mattress, you who are entirely harmless. Ghostly notional beings: I see you have finally taken on bodily form to rap on the wall of your wicked, wicked neighbour.

The music started up again.

7

Yeo Sonyeo turned off the stove and opened the window. Cool air threaded through the stuffy gas-shot air, creating a light breeze. The blinds swayed, gently scattering a sooty layer of caked dust. The low buildings towards Jongno were visible through the window. Here and there, last month's snow still glistened on the flat dingy roofs, and there wasn't a single cat basking in the winter sun. Yeo Sonyeo returned to his chair and picked up the newspaper again.

Yeo Sonyeo didn't like the current mayor. Though younger than Yeo Sonyeo by about ten years he appeared at least five years older, and always seemed so certain of his convictions. Yeo Sonyeo was a person with convictions too, but his own somehow paled beside the mayor's as if his faith wasn't quite as good or as pure. This frustrated Yeo Sonyeo. He resumed reading with a despondent air. The article said the mayor's plan to restore the walk deck would move forward regardless. The plan was to connect Sewoon and Cheonggye Markets by extending the deck over Cheonggyecheon — the stream that flowed between the two buildings — and thereby invigorate the heart of the city through a greater influx of people to the area; and to foster technicians in order to revitalise its surroundings and reinstate Sewoon Market as a new, or

74   dd's Umbrella

renewed, landmark. As Yeo Sonyeo understood it, the primary goal of the project was to increase foot traffic. The number of people passing by. And as they passed by... But would it work? Would it bring people back? So many shops had closed for lack of customers. Yeo Sonyeo found he couldn't summon much enthusiasm for the project. People passing by? Hmph. As if anything here would attract the attention of children with their cotton candy and balloons or of youngsters out on a date. As if they'd even care. Yeo Sonyeo couldn't picture adult folk visiting his shop, a five-year-old with ketchup down their fancy clothes in tow, to discuss vintage audio systems with him. Or he could, but the image seemed to exist in the realm of possibility only as that, an imagined scenario. And what of the scenario that a young couple out for a stroll along the third-floor walk deck would stop to check out heat sinks, resistors, ICs, DC motors, loudspeaker units, and transformers?

Of course, a general increase in traffic would generate more trade, even if it was a different type of trade from the current one. Yeo Sonyeo looked down at the deck from his window. Initially designed to be part of the ambitious plan for Sewoon — as grand as its name, which spelled out a vision for all the world's (se, 世) energy (woon, 運) congregating here — the elevated walkway had never been realised according to the blueprint. It was only partially constructed to begin with, was later further disconnected, and now stood in the cold, pale light of the February sun, once again talked up as a linchpin of yet another grand ambitious scheme. Uniform box stalls like the ones housing shoe repairers in street corners lined the deck. Most were closed, and in one where the door was open, a young man sat with his back to the sun, playing Solitaire on his computer. A short standing sign placed in the shade announced the sale of Viagra, cigarettes, and security cameras. In any case, if foot traffic did increase and business picked up in turn, shop owners were liable to hike the rent. According to the movers and shakers behind this grand enterprise, this revitalisation project as they called it, technicians like Yeo Sonyeo were to provide, no, they were to *be* the project's 'content'. But technicians and tradespeople were also tenants at the end of the day, and if rent prices went up few retailers would be able to stay put, what with the high concentration of small businesses in the area. It could prove the final blow. The market may survive, but that doesn't mean I will, thought Yeo Sonyeo.

The newspaper rustled in the wind. Yeo Sonyeo folded it, twice, so that the article he wanted to read faced him. It detailed the announcement of the Sewoon Market Revitalisation Plan. The word *regeneration*, which was repeated five times in the article, bothered Yeo Sonyeo. Regenerate what exactly? And why?

Yeo Sonyeo wanted answers to these questions and wondered if the project's planners did too. As far as he could tell, the energy of the entire world was already gathered here at Sewoon: the predictable linking of present to future; the reality that fell short of the ideal; the grandiose, charmless exterior; the folk who were mostly overlooked by the times, then and now, but who nonetheless had persevered and eked out a living, and in so doing had defined an era — and were now relegated to the dregs of another era. The swindlers, the crooks, the liars, including Yeo Sonyeo himself, but only the pettiest sort, of negligible scale, and who in that pettiness had washed up here like the regular nobodies they were. His neighbours, all... As far as Yeo Sonyeo could gather, *this* was the world's energy. If they wanted to really and truly revitalise

76 dd's Umbrella

the place, breathe life into it, this is what they had to show, never mind their posturing. Those who said they wanted to revitalise it needed to know what it was they were revitalising. They needed to know, *really* know, and they needed to do it right... Which meant for a start that the stories of everyone who'd lived and worked and breathed here should be displayed for all to see, at minimum. Detailing what illnesses they had suffered, how seldom they'd travelled in their lives, and accounts of their families too — meeting the families in person so they could tell the story of the children, which schools they'd attended and what jobs they'd had, what percentage of them had wound up with irregular work — surely they should look into all that as well. They ought to produce a great big scroll of these stories and unroll it over every inch of this massive site of commerce, cover it from top to bottom and inside and out with the life and words of each of these neighbours.

Yeo Sonyeo thought about the structure that had appeared a week ago. Last Wednesday, he'd arrived in the morning to the strangest sight. In the middle of the fifth-floor atrium someone had heaped various junk and scrap-metal objects, from monitors, fans, and old telephones to tattered loudspeakers, then strewn moss and flowering branches over the whole thing. They'd managed to string some Christmas lights over it, and the clear skylight cast the whole thing in a whitish glow. Yeo Sonyeo immediately thought of seonangdang, the stone heaps dedicated to village deities. But it also looked as though some giant mysterious creature had devoured and shat out an entire junk shop overnight. What on earth, Yeo Sonyeo wondered. Clumps of earth and green bits were visible here and there, and as a matter of fact, the heap did resemble a tomb that had only partially been covered with topsoil and turf. Why anyone would dream of leaving this in someone else's front yard was beyond him. Yeo Sonyeo circled around the installation, frowning, and headed to his shop. Not long after, a young man and a woman, probably college students, walked into the shop and handed him a piece of paper, saying it was an invitation. There was to be a gathering to mark the opening of an exhibition as well as the commencement of the revitalisation project that afternoon. Yeo Sonyeo couldn't be less interested. It'd be a party of their own, they'd snap a few photos and disappear: the same old tune.

As expected, people he'd never laid eyes on before assembled in the fourth-floor hall that afternoon, fussed about, clicked their cameras, then were gone. Yeo Sonyeo didn't venture outside until he was sure the hall was empty, only to find the installation was still there. Noticing a piece of paper on it, Yeo Sonyeo stepped closer, and read: DO NOT TOUCH. He was appalled. The cheek of it, he thought, ordering us around when the people most likely to read this note are the ones supposedly providing the living, breathing *content* of all your grand plans, people like *me*, yes that's right, *I'm* the *content*, you shits… I've been here right from the beginning, forty years we've been the blood running through this place and no one thinks to ask a single question of us, of me, and *that's* your project? Well, I've no use for it, for any of it. Yeo Sonyeo lit a cigarette and circled the installation. This is truly… the most magnificent symbol, he thought. Its unforeseen abruptness and its utter disconnect summed up the situation beautifully. Not that any of this was new. Yeo Sonyeo considered the city's municipal projects, whether this one or any other, as nothing but sham conspiracies. Public bodies allocated funding and the

78 dd's Umbrella

projects were carried out, that was all. Nothing to do with me. None of it is ever done with my participation, my involvement, no, I'm excluded from it all. The same old tune. This symbolic piece had zero context — the context of Yeo Sonyeo, of shops nos. 564, 568, 531, 540, and 536. The people behind it had no idea, knew nothing of this context. Why else would they deposit a seonangdang in someone else's yard, as if they're trying to chase ghosts away? Am I a ghost?

With a bitter taste in his mouth, Yeo Sonyeo put away the newspaper and got up to close the window. His gums ached. It seemed the third implant was acting up again. Yeo Sonyeo cursed the dentist again for ramming the screw and implant in there. He adjusted the tuner on the radio in search of a cleaner sound. From his shop he could only catch the channel on 91.9FM. All other stations were fuzzy with static. Yeo Sonyeo was convinced that this was because the market was located at the heart of the city with its abundance of radio signals, and because the age of the building impeded good reception. Installing a device on the roof would help, but the caretakers disallowed that. They argued that shelling out money to install a device just so a few ancient radio players would have better reception was not only unreasonable, it also hurt the aesthetics of the building. When people dropped by his shop to have their radios repaired, Yeo Sonyeo would ask them where they lived. He'd ask if they had good radio reception there and would feel genuine envy when he heard that they did. It was his dream to live out his last days in the hills or in some remote village with fresh air and water and quiet all around, but the one precondition was access to a radio signal. There had to be good reception. For now, the radio was hissing again with static, despite the clear weather.

Hwang 79

For two days now, there'd been a ruckus downstairs about Yoon Seono. Yoon Seono was an elderly man who'd started frequenting the audio shops a few years back and had become quite chummy with the shopkeeps, sharing a meal or a drink with them on occasion. The audio folk liked him. He didn't overstay his welcome, he was polite, he dressed in simple but expensive clothes, and though he seemed knowledgeable he never acted like it, and he wasn't stingy either. He hadn't been to any of the shops for some months though and a few people had started wondering about his health. But just last week, Yoon Seono had come by Baek San's shop and stayed to chat for ten minutes, after which Baek noticed an item was missing. He immediately pointed his finger at Yoon Seono, but others were reluctant to believe him. If forced to say which of these two men they were less likely to believe, most would hands down name Baek. A seller of second-hand audio systems, Baek San was a big man with a booming voice and laugh, and his face could go from laughing to menacing and back again in mere seconds. He was shameless, he swindled everyone, and he was entirely unconcerned with business ethics. He'd think nothing of buying a second-hand stereo in need of serious repair on the cheap, selling it at an inflated price, and then saddling the hapless buyer with the cost of fixing it. Yeo Sonyeo had been ripped off a few times too, but when it suited him, Baek would show up again with pleasantries and brazenly ask Yeo Sonyeo to repair this or that, then conveniently neglect to pay him. This happened repeatedly. Though Yeo Sonyeo tolerated Baek San as one of the numerous elements that composed the microcosm of this four-decades-old electronics market, he didn't trust Baek San one bit.

80   dd's Umbrella

But the security footage seemed to confirm the theft. An old device of no real commercial value had sat atop the pile of amps outside, and Yoon Seono had not only nicked it as he left the shop, he'd been caught on camera. They all gathered to watch the footage, but still couldn't believe it. Because it made no sense. They were sure of the man's character, for one, and they couldn't fathom why someone who owned several McIntosh stereos would take an ancient CD player priced at ₩100,000. And as everyone knew, if that was the asking price at Baek San Audio, it had to be practically worthless. A husk, its innards sure to be gutted. He may as well have thrown it out, which of course was why he kept it outside, and Yoon Seono had to know this. And who steals a crummy machine headed for the scrapyard, especially when they own several pieces of high-end vintage equipment? What possible use to him is a CD player? The vendors played back the footage a few times, exchanged baffled looks, then set about pacifying Baek San — who was threatening to take the footage to the police — and attempting a mediation.

Yeo Sonyeo was given the recap later that evening:

So the Hanilsa sajang made the call, since the two of them are so chummy. Apparently, Yoon Seono answered as if nothing was up. And when Hanilsa asked point-blank if he'd maybe taken something from the shop, he pretended to know nothing about it. So Hanilsa brought up the CCTV footage, and that's when instead of answering he asked, all calm like, Did you see?

Did you see?

Oh, you saw?

Then he finally admitted to it. Yes, I took it, he said. Hanilsa asked if he'd needed a CD player, but he said no. And the whole time he's completely unfazed, like all this is nothing. Hanilsa got spooked then and said, Well let's not turn this into a bigger problem, will you send a hundred thousand and we'll say that settles it?

Of course Baek San butted in then to say he wanted a hundred and fifty.

And he got it too.

Yoon Seono wired the money that same afternoon.

None of it makes sense.

Why'd you reckon he did it?

Not for lack of money, that's for sure.

Maybe he didn't have any cash on him?

But he wouldn't need a cheap CD player in the first place.

Maybe it's kleptomania?

Who gets kleptomania overnight?

Might happen.

Could be Alzheimer's.

Nah, we'd have noticed.

Why then?

Why indeed.

So they wondered and asked, as if by repeating the question they would arrive at an answer.

The way I see it, Yeo Sonyeo said to d when the others had left, the old man was getting us back. Getting his revenge on us all.

Yeo Sonyeo recalled how in the security footage Yoon Seono had looked about him before picking up the CD player and striding out of the frame. According to Baek San, the older man had said he'd been out of sorts for a while due to a bad cold, and his face did look rather gaunt on the screen.

82   dd's Umbrella

Yeo Sonyeo had developed a relationship with Yoon Seono over the years, sharing an occasional dinner or a chat. Yoon would smile cryptically when anyone asked him what he'd done before retirement, but over time he did share certain facts about his life: he had a son who was a professor at a university outside of Seoul, and he owned and lived in a hanok with a yard in Bukchon. One day he spoke about his plans to have a small waterfall put in his yard. Later he'd come by Yeo Sonyeo's shop with a plan of the watercourse, drawn with a felt tip on a huge sheet of paper folded over many times. The watercourse was shaped like a Western pear, tapering at the top and rounded at the bottom. The little broccoli-like scribbles along the course were the rosebushes and trees in his yard. He wanted the waterfall for its music. To hear, in summer, water stream past the blooming white rosebushes, encircle the maple, reach the knee-high drop beside the cherry tree and cascade down, tumbling over the black rocks below. The sound of flowing water could be heavenlier than any music, and it was a long-held dream of his to lie out on the maru and listen to it for hours on end, a dream he finally meant to realise from the comfort of his own home.

But when Yeo Sonyeo asked about the waterfall sometime later, the older man's expression had turned sour. Yes, he'd had it installed, but when he turned on the tap there was an awful din, and now, because drawing water out of the pipe caused such a racket, he mostly left the thing dry and empty. He said he was waiting for rain, for the big torrential rains. Hearing this Yeo Sonyeo thought to himself that while rain would allow the waterfall to work naturally, the sound of a downpour was bound to drown out the gentle music Yoon had hoped for. He kept this to himself and said instead, Lucky you, to live out all

Hwang 83

your dreams. At this Yoon Seono's pale face had contorted, from what might have been barely suppressed revulsion or contempt. Or perhaps anger. A surge of emotions flooded the man's face, and so rapidly, that the face appeared much too small and narrow to hold it all. Yeo Sonyeo could still see it. But Yoon Seono had quickly resumed his usual gentle expression, and patting Yeo Sonyeo on the shoulder had suggested they go get some galbitang. Yeo Sonyeo never forgot that face though.

Now he wondered if the waterfall was real. There was something about that look, the way Yoon Seono had glanced at the security camera before taking the CD player. Yeo Sonyeo didn't know where the man lived. Where his failed project was supposed to be. Yoon Seono had said he had a problem with one of his McIntoshes, had asked Yeo Sonyeo if he would drop by one day to look at it as it was too heavy to transport. Yeo Sonyeo had happily agreed, but Yoon Seono had never actually extended an invitation. So he didn't know. No one did. For the simple reason that no one had ever been to the man's place. Not a single one of us has any idea where and how that man lives, Yeo Sonyeo thought. Six years we've known him and no one has a clue.

He said to d, I can't believe he would do such a thing, but I have to, now that I've seen it. The thing is, though, that the more I believe it the more it looks to me like he was getting us back... As if he wanted to reveal himself, to show us how wrong we were about him, to taunt us for believing what we believed... Why did he feel the need to get back at us? Well, the more I think about it, the more it seems like it's because he's on his last legs. Who knows what's been going on in his life, but I think he must have had death on his mind for

84 dd's Umbrella

whatever reason, his own death... That's the only motive that makes sense.

Yeo Sonyeo pictured Yoon Seono's pale face and asked d if they had ever thought about the afterlife.

No, d answered.

d was sitting in their usual chair, as they often did in the evenings now, looking over at Yeo Sonyeo with glinting black eyes. They wore a thin, quilted jacket and had a work cap slung over their left knee, and was crumpling up the wrapper of the steamed bun they'd just gobbled up. Their face was sedate, haggard, drawn. Yeo Sonyeo remembered how d had worn that exact expression when they lugged the stereo back to the shop, barely a week after they'd purchased it. They'd brought everything back and asked if they could leave it at the shop and stop by now and then to listen to it. This was such an unusual request that it took a while for Yeo Sonyeo to comprehend what was being asked.

Can you what?

What I mean is... could I leave the stereo with you here and come to the shop to listen to it until I find a suitable place to keep it?

Could you... well, you've already brought it here so what's the point of asking? Hang on though, you want to *listen* to it? *Here*? Yeo Sonyeo had asked again, and that was when d had looked at him with the expression they wore now. Yeo Sonyeo had tut-tutted, then gone about making space in the next room. He'd been using it as storage space, having removed the thin single-panel door that separated it from the room where he worked. Boxes of amps delivered to his shop sat to one corner of the space. d cleared that all up and placed their stereo there. And from that day on they began to show up at night to listen to music, sometimes just the one song and at other times until it got very late. Yeo Sonyeo tended to turn the volume up mercilessly when testing amps he was repairing, but d didn't seem to mind. They didn't startle at the sudden loud blasts from the worktable. They sat unperturbed, completely wrapped up in whatever music they were listening to. After a while, Yeo Sonyeo stopped noticing d, even forgot their presence. Grumbling at burned circuitry or turning around to reach for something, he'd startle at the sight of d sitting in the corner with their face to the stereo. They appeared oblivious to their surroundings. Sometimes it looked like they were sitting in silence, despite the music, as if they were in a separate world altogether.

Hmm, Yeo Sonyeo said now, rolling his eyes this way and that. You've never imagined what it might be like?

No.

Not ever?

No.

How curious, Yeo Sonyeo thought. Doesn't everyone wonder about death at some point or another? Well, he said, as for me, something happened to me once that makes me think I've already had a glimpse of it.

Three or four years ago, I was having a drink here with some of the men from downstairs, he told d. We were drinking soju and makgeolli with pig's trotters and some rice cake someone had brought as anju. A while past midnight, it must have been nearly one o'clock, there was a power cut. We could see the lights over in Jongno-1-ga out of that window, but this entire area was pitch black. Well, what can you do? We went on drinking, fumbling for bottles and plates in the dark. We could

86 dd's Umbrella

make some things out; I could see the other's profiles, even make out their expressions in the moonlight. At one point I must have dozed off, paper cup in hand, because I was shaken awake. The five of them were smirking. Let's play, they said. Play? I said. I'm done playing, now I need to sleep so leave me be, but they wouldn't hear of it. Come on, they insisted. Come on and what, I asked, and they said, Let's get out of here. The whole building's dark anyway, so let's go play hide and seek. It's the middle of the night, I said, there's no one about, we can't, but they said that was why it'd be perfect, because nobody's about. Come on, let's do it, like when we were kids, might as well while we're drunk. So I said Fine, fine, who's going to be it first, and they said You, you're it, we'll go out and hide, you come and look for us in a minute. And off they went. While I stayed behind, being it.

But I couldn't remember the words you're supposed to say when you're it. Was it *Hey fox, hey fox*? Or *Dead or alive, you better hide, I can see the hair on your head*? I mumbled whatever I could think of, then went out to look for them. It was ridiculous, playing hide and seek at my age with a group of grey men. But you know what? It was fun. Maybe it was the booze and the warm glow in my stomach, but yes, I had a laugh. It was dark still. No light except the gleaming moon, a faint bluish glimmering above the skylight that made the hall look vast and the shadows inky, and I thought, Sheesh, I hadn't realised how immense this space is. It surprised me. The hall couldn't have *appeared* bigger or darker only that night. Anyway, the five of them were nowhere to be seen. I searched all over the fifth floor, but nothing. Not them, not anyone. Thinking they must have sneaked downstairs, I made my way down.

Normally the fire door's bolted shut at night but that night it was open, maybe because of the power cut. I walked around the fourth floor thinking they've got to be here somewhere, but again I was alone on the entire unlit floor. It was uncanny. The longer I wandered, the stranger I felt. Gwangjin Electronics, Jigu Electronics, Yeon Sound, Bando Electronics, the Classics Company, Ehwa Electronics... Familiar shops and corridors I've walked past every day for decades, but it all felt different. The shop signs, the insides of shops seen through glass walls, all of it I'd seen the previous day and the day before that, even earlier that same day, but somehow they all looked unfamiliar. No sign of anyone, just the dark and my footsteps echoing like a stone dropped down a dry well... Come out come out wherever you are, I chanted as I walked round and round, but there wasn't a soul about. So, this is what the afterlife's like, I thought. The thought just came to me, that this was a sort of preview, as if I'd simply slipped, silently and unwittingly, from this life into the afterlife, from this world into that in the blink of an eye. That this, here, was my afterlife...

Yeo Sonyeo trailed off, and in the ensuing silence heard d say, in a barely audible voice, 25 February, 1983. Where were you on that day?

On that day thirty-two years ago, d said, I was on the west coast. The tide was out and the brown mud flat was wet and hard and cold. The grown-ups and the younger cousins were all there, though I don't remember what the occasion was. Some family gathering. I'd been mucking about in the mud with my tiny shovel, trying to dig up clams and whatnot, and had just stood up. Still holding on to the shovel or the pail, I don't know which. I think there was a light breeze. We were

88 dd's Umbrella

all looking up at the sky. The adults were obviously panicked, I remember that. All the kids stared up at the sky to see what the adults were looking at. But there wasn't anything there. Except the sky, of course. We could hear sirens. Ringing out up and down the coast. As you know, 25 February, 1983, was the day North Korean Air Force Lieutenant Lee Woong-pyung defected to the South in a Russian MiG fighter jet. The whole country was in uproar and rumours went round saying this was only the beginning of a military campaign by North Korea. My memory of that day is summed up by that scene on the beach. I heard some older folk discussing the defection recently, which is what brought the moment back, though I can't tell if it's a memory I've always had or one I've made up. Either way, the scene itself is very vivid, and very still. It's suspended, like the long wail of a siren.

When I think of death, this is what comes to mind. Moments that definitely happened or seem much too real not to have happened. Moments that are all in the past and on pause. As if they have no ties to the present and are destined to remain cut off and unrelated and forever without an after... Forever frozen in time. Even now, I feel it. When I'm sitting still as I'm doing now but also when I move, when I think but also when I'm not thinking, I sense death. This very static now. It's so inert, I can't imagine what comes after and I don't wonder about it either. The now is already here anyway. It just slips in, as you put it. Slip, and there it is... We don't need to imagine it. So no, I don't wonder about a world after this one. When I think about the past or the present, it is always death. And death is death, not a divide between this and that world, and all death can only ever be categorised as one of two. At least that's what I think. It's either witnessed or it's unwitnessed. Isn't it?

But did you know, d continued, that the reason Lieutenant Lee Woong-pyung fled was because he was disillusioned? He said he came across an empty ramyeon wrapper, produced in the South, while walking on a beach. The wrapper had a sentence on it that said *defective products will be replaced or refunded by your local retailer.* That's when he realised that there were places in the South that had ramyeon to sell by the hundreds and more, and he felt so betrayed by and disillusioned with the state that he decided to defect. When I heard this story, I envied him. What I wouldn't give to be in that seat, joystick in hand, headed straight for my destination, I thought. To be Lieutenant Lee Woong-pyung as he flies his music-filled jet to the border, the radio blaring out South Korean pop songs as he travels across the vast, empty sky. Suspended in air, a single flimsy sheet of metal the only thing separating him from death, and yet, in that moment, he was, without a doubt, headed away from disillusion. Towards its opposite. And he got to experience it — escape.

Unlike me.

I don't even have a place to head towards if I were to escape.

8

d kept Park Jobae's book on the floor by the bed and would open it before falling asleep. The yellow ribbon marker had been placed in the middle of the book, the brown one towards the back. d had never seen a book with two markers before. At first d thought it must be a production error, but the different colours and the fact that the ribbons were attached side by side suggested intent. Considering the bulk of the book, this made sense. dd had probably read up to the spot marked by the yellow ribbon, d thought, since it was their habit on finishing a book to place the marker either before the first page or after the final page of the book.

The yellow ribbon lay in the furrow between pages 246 and 247. The last sentence on page 246 was: *This is only the shallow refuge of the person who does not yet know what he is doing.* The first sentence on page 247: *In fact, the opposite is true.*

d wondered where dd had stopped reading, the page to the left or the right of the marker, and at which line of which paragraph. d turned the page. The paper was thick but light and somewhat rough. d began reading from the top of the right-hand page. The book wasn't as warm as other objects were against their skin. Beginning that day, d made a habit of returning home from work and reading a few lines or pages of

92   dd's Umbrella

the book before turning in. It wasn't the subject of the book
per se that interested them so much as the physical weight of it,
the way it smelled, the colour of its letters; these material
aspects of the book helped lull d to sleep. Each night d
resumed reading from the page they'd marked the night before,
and each night moved the brown ribbon to wherever they'd
read to that night. Eventually, the brown ribbon made it back
to the very last page of the book, at which point d opened the
book to its first page and started reading towards the middle of
the book marked by the yellow ribbon. *This is only the shallow
refuge of the person who does not yet know what he is doing.* When
they reached this last sentence on page 246, d placed the
ribbon markers together and closed the book.

They packed the book in their rucksack and took it with
them to work the next day. In the evening they clocked out a
little earlier than usual. After stuffing their sweaty work clothes
into the rucksack, d hesitated, then stuck the book under their
arm and headed to Myeongdong to look for Park Jobae. It was
a Thursday on a mildly cold spring night. Park Jobae was still
there, selling albums and socks in Myeongdong's tourist-packed
streets from a modest cart wedged in between a cart selling
pan-fried potatoes and another selling T-shirts. Vendors called
out in Chinese and Japanese above the din of overlapping
music. Park Jobae sat, hands between his thighs, staring off
towards Toegyero. It's been a while, d said. Park Jobae looked
vacantly at d. I've come to return this, d said, holding out the
book. Park Jobae frowned as he took the book. Huh, he said.
Then: Yeah, this is mine. Park Jobae said he'd lent it to dd a
long time ago. dd had come to see him in Myeongdong one
day, he said, to invite him over. For the housewarming... the
two of you had just moved into an oktop. Yes, d nodded.

Where's dd? asked Park Jobae. Oh, they couldn't make it, d answered. I see, said Park Jobae. d looked at Park Jobae, at the brown book on his thigh. They noticed a long mark, a fingerprint on the cover. Whose is that? d wondered. Mine? dd's? Park Jobae's? An ambulance sped along Toegyero, sirens blaring. Have you had dinner? Park Jobae asked. d shook their head. I've got to be somewhere tonight so I'm closing up early, Park Jobae said, why don't we grab a bowl of noodles?

d waited at Hoehyeon intersection while Park Jobae went to park his cart. The book was under their arm, as Park Jobae had asked them to hold on to it. Park Jobae appeared on the other side of the crossing, towards Daeyeongak Building. The light changed and he strolled over, hands in his trouser pockets and a large, heavy-looking gym bag on one shoulder. They went to a noodle shop Park Jobae knew in Sogongno, ordered a bowl each, sprinkled ribbons of dried laver and chopped spring onion, and began eating. d kept Park Jobae's book on their thigh as they ate. Park Jobae talked about how much he'd missed gim when he lived in Italy as a student. I love gim, he said, sprinkling another spoonful of ribboned gim over his half-eaten noodles. Once, when I was a kid, I secretly ate an entire pack of dried gim, he went on. But I couldn't keep it down of course, and my family panicked thinking I was vomiting blood...

Do you mind? We're eating.

Yeah, sorry.

d scraped at the few noodle strands left in their bowl and asked where in Italy Park Jobae had lived. In the north, Park Jobae answered. Down south they have a lot of swamps. And the mafia, of course. I hate humidity and shootings so I never set foot in southern Italy, he said. Then Park Jobae confessed that he'd studied architecture for a year in Milan but had gotten

94 dd's Umbrella

very poor grades. He said it was because he'd lived in students' quarters that were maintained by monks and had been harassed by nightmarish roommates and bedbugs; he still had the scars from the bite marks on his back and thighs. Park Jobae's face looked bloodless. His thick wavy hair was greasy, and his forehead, nose, and cheeks were covered in freckles. d tried to remember how Park Jobae had looked as a child. Well, his adult face was longer, but otherwise he hadn't changed much. The second finger of his right hand was a little crooked, maybe because he had a habit of twisting it when he wasn't speaking. My roommates... I guess you could say they bit me too, Park Jobae continued, because they ratted me out to the monks, told them about my private life and took turns complaining and saying they didn't want me as a roommate. Told people behind my back that I kept going on about revolutions, that I was constantly hassling them with talk of politics and the need for a revolution...

You're interested in revolutions? d asked. Park Jobae ate a piece of kkakdugi and answered that he liked revolutionaries. He liked them for believing they could change the world, for actually trying to effect change and in some cases even succeeding. It's admirable, he said. I was especially drawn to the interwar and post-WWII artists. What those revolutionary artists achieved even as the ground was being ripped out from underneath them and the foundations were being destroyed leaving nothing but a bottomless pit, how they overcame that groundlessness — I found that intriguing.

Park Jobae and d left the noodle shop and stood for a while looking down Sogongno. The road was nearly empty. d made to hand over the book, but Park Jobae glanced at it and said, No need. You keep it.

Can I? d asked.

I don't read books like that anymore, Park Jobae said. Why bother reading about revolutions happening elsewhere as if they're blowhard heroic accounts? What's the point.

Adjusting his gym bag, he said he was headed to Gwanghwamun and asked which way d was headed. There was a bus near the Donghwa Duty Free Building in Gwanghwamun that would take d back to their room. Shall we head to Gwanghwamun then? Park Jobae said. The two of them started walking towards Plaza Hotel.

They followed Sogongno past Plaza Hotel and crossed into Seoul Plaza. A big stage had been installed to the east of the grassy plaza outside City Hall, and a large number of people were milling about the lawn. They seemed to be moving away from the stage and heading to Sejong-daero. A large illuminated replica of a ship was suspended over the stage. d recognised the ship's blue hull and white upper half.

Today's the one-year anniversary, Park Jobae said. One year since the sinking. He said he had known about today's commemoration but had decided to stop by the memorial altar in Gwanghwamun later as he couldn't give up on his evening trade altogether; now thanks to d's visit he was headed there a bit early. d saw people walk past with white chrysanthemums. Above, dozens of big flags flapped from poles carried by different groups amid the crowd. Some people had brought picnic mats and rucksacks as if they were headed on a daytrip, others were in suits and business attire as though they'd come directly from the surrounding office buildings. Traffic on Sejong-daero had been diverted, and people walked down the thoroughfare towards Gwanghwamun. Park Jobae and d followed behind.

96   dd's Umbrella

As they approached Gwanghwamun the crowd increased and the flow slowed. The people who'd gone ahead were stopped at the junction by Cheonggye Plaza. Police vehicles were parked across Sejong-daero to form a barricade, the horizontal blue lines and POLICE signs facing the throng. The road was wet and people in raincoats or holding up umbrellas were demanding the police remove the car wall and let them through. There was an acrid smell. The air was heavy with particles that stung and irritated the throat's lining. d saw the round helmets gazing down at the crowd from the tops of the trucks forming the barricade. It was impossible to reach Gwanghwamun.

Park Jobae suggested crossing over to Gwanghwamun via the underground passage that connected to the subway station. They found an entrance to the passage, but it was already blocked. Riot police in fluorescent yellow-green jackets and helmets stood in rows down the stairs. People stranded below or above ground and unable to exit or access the subway station, were complaining to the police, who remained unresponsive. Long lines of police buses stretched along the road, obstructing pavements and cutting off access to bus stops, now rendered useless. What now, they wondered. At the bottom of the stairs to the station, a man was protesting, How the fuck am I supposed to get home? Park Jobae and d stood behind the cluster of people at the top of the stairs and listened as they shouted at the police, protesting the obstruction of citizens' free movement. What will you do? Park Jobae asked. d said they could cross the river on foot. You want to head home then? Park Jobae asked. d was unable to answer straight away. There was a commotion in front of the Finance Center Building. People and flags were moving towards Cheonggyecheon-ro.

Come, walk with me, Park Jobae said.

I left Italy just before the general election, Park Jobae told d. I told my Italian friends they'd be finished if Berlusconi was elected. I kept telling them, but not one of them listened. I arrived back here before the results were announced. Why? You mean why did I come back? What do you think? Because I ran out of money, of course. So when Silvio Berlusconi, the tycoon and founding member of Forza Italia, won the 2008 general election to serve his fourth term as prime minister, I told my friends in Italy, I called each of my former roommates, and I told them, you're all fucked now, wait and you'll see, you'll see. Because Berlusconi was, roughly speaking, Italy's version of Lee Myung-bak. We had Lee Myung-bak, they had Berlusconi. We're the same, I told them, you lot over there and us here, we're all in the same boat. You'll see, we're all finished, we're all going to pot in the exact same way. I warned them, but they wouldn't let go of their ideas, all they had to say was, Oh please. Leave me alone you shit, was the extent of their response. And now look at them. They've been truly fucked over. As for us... I honestly believed electing Lee Myung-bak would be our rock bottom...

Park Jobae said he planned to circumvent the phalanxes of police and head to Jongno through Cheonggyecheon-ro, after which he'd pass through Jongno to reach Gwanghwamun. But Cheonggyecheon-ro, it turned out, was already lined left and right with police buses. Each parked bus had its engine running and the air was thick with exhaust. Park Jobae and d found an opening in the barricade near Mojeon-gyo but seeing the tight cordons of police in riot helmets lying in wait, they decided to walk a bit farther along. There were people behind

98   dd's Umbrella

them, it didn't make sense to turn back and go against the current, the only option was to continue along the narrow pavement, along the white expanse of police buses that stretched on. People chanted for their right to march peacefully. Across the stream and walkway, large groups of people progressed under various flags and banners.

Park Jobae talked about how he'd shifted from selling pop albums to socks. No one listens to CDs anymore, do they, he said. The odd Chinese and Japanese tourists might come in search of K-pop albums, but socks are what sell, socks printed with the faces of pop idols or animal characters. Park Jobae's laces kept coming undone, and every so often the two of them stopped by the fence along the stream, stepping aside to let people pass. The third time this happened, d reached out for Park Jobae's gym bag. Park Jobae hurriedly tied his laces while d waited, the bag slung on their shoulder. It was even heavier than it had seemed. Park Jobae inhaled loudly, straightened his back and stood up. Handing over the bag, d asked why it was so heavy. Park Jobae patted it and said all his earthly possessions were inside it. A few rare albums from his personal collection that he displayed on his cart as samples, a bit of cash, a gold necklace, the books he was reading at the moment, some underwear, and toiletries. He had water and energy bars in there too, so if ever there was an emergency this bag was all he needed, he could survive a few days on what was inside.

What kind of emergency?

War or radiation leakage.

d and Park Jobae stood and waited for the crowd, which by now had slowed considerably, to move ahead. As they walked Park Jobae glanced down periodically to make sure his laces hadn't come undone.

Hwang 99

Everyone here acts as if those things will never happen, but that's exactly how they occur in the first place, he continued. Exactly when everyone least expects it and precisely because we've stopped paying attention. That's when you see people evaporate into thin air, leaving their rooms and belongings behind, everything intact, to be discovered much later. Even now, in parts of Europe, they still come across rooms like that in old homes, big villas. When I was in Italy, I'd see stories on the news about abandoned homes being discovered in Paris or in London, empty rooms that lay undiscovered for seventy years because people fled them during the war and never returned. As for the objects they left behind, they're like spectres. Open perfume bottles and powder puffs on dressing tables, a shawl hurriedly thrown over a stuffed ostrich, tables with the remnants of someone's last tea, boots cast off by a fireplace that's long grown dark and cold... And these get you thinking, they really get you thinking about *before*, the period before whatever occurred occurred, those seconds or minutes or hours, sometimes days or weeks or years prior to the event... About how whoever used to inhabit that room disappeared in the blink of an eye, or fled for good to some other place, and how unforeseen and out of the blue these erasures were.

They were crossing Gwangtong-gyo now and at Gwang-gyo crossroads they tried to turn left, but the street there, Woojeongguk-ro, was already bottlenecked by police buses. Helmeted, shield-carrying police officers stood in cordons in front of the vehicles, while people in business attire gestured at a building nearby, asking why they were being impeded from entering the pub *right there*. Park Jobae and d stopped to watch for a bit before continuing on. Jongno-8-gil was also cordoned

100   dd's Umbrella

off towards Bosingak, and Jongno-8-gil was jam-packed with riot police. Where does this blockade end? Park Jobae muttered. It looks like we're completely trapped. He coughed as he'd been doing periodically from the exhaust spewed by the riot buses.

Seeing Jongno-12-gil was also blocked, Park Jobae and d went down to the stream. They'd hoped to avoid the fumes, but the stream itself was blanketed in white smoke. Fuck it, Park Jobae said, we should have stayed up at street level. But he seemed oddly elated too. Spitting out foamy saliva, he slung the gym bag over his back and walked on, his hands in his trouser pockets and his strides long. The moon and the stars were invisible, but the night was bright. The water gleamed black as it flowed towards Dongdaemun, and on either side of it willows in new leaf and blossoming cherry flowers cast beautiful shadows in the light. The flag-carrying people on the other side of Cheonggyecheon started to chant:

Scrap the Sewol Bill.

Scrap the Sewol Bill.

Step Down Park Geun-hye.

Salvage Sewol Ferry Now.

Police arriving on the scene started to file onto Jangtonggyo. Protestors who'd been heading north towards Jongno found themselves confronted. Park Jobae and d stopped to observe. Shields and helmets flashed under the streetlights. Shouts rang out as scuffling ensued on the bridge, and there was a commotion of stamping and dragging feet.

The signs are always there, Park Jobae said.

What signs?

d turned to face Park Jobae, their eyes bleary from the exhaust. Emergency is another word for the extraordinary

Hwang 101

event, those times when something out of the ordinary occurs, Park Jobae explained, but the extraordinary always manifests in the everyday. There are indications. Sudden is never as sudden as we make it out to be.

When we say something's happened out of nowhere, we're actually admitting to feigned ignorance, our refusal to look at the everyday, he went on. When in fact they're all around us, all of the signs are right there in broad daylight. Think about wars. Every war has a context. Radiation? We wouldn't have leaks without the portent that is the nuclear power plant. The same applies to what's happening now. For me, the present is always an omen. This moment right now, it's like the interwar years. The period between the first and second world wars was full of portents. I can feel the same rumblings now. I can feel the world's about to break again. Yes, it's a kind of premonition, but it feels very concrete, very certain. The world's fucked again, and this time it's going to be decisive... I can feel it. Just look at the art produced between those two wars, especially the music. Classical, jazz, whatever, you can hear the artists singing and playing as if they're facing the end of the world. I think they definitely felt something. The same thing as I feel now, a sense of the coming catastrophe in the air around us. What we're facing is very similar, we're on the verge, the before... and that's why I think it's better to have scenes like this. Park Jobae pointed to the bridge with his chin.

Look at this. Look how transparent and how fucked up it is. The fuckedupness out in the open for all to see. I say this is infinitely better than imploding in quiet denial.

d and Park Jobae attempted to get back to street level when they reached Supyo-gyo, but police filed up the narrow steps

102   dd's Umbrella

leading to the road. Others who had also walked down to the stream were expressing their indignation, but the police made no response, nor did they show any inclination to let them up the stairs. A woman who had been watching the situation flopped down on the bottom step, removed her shoes, and started massaging her stockinged calves. Some people jumped up the retaining wall and climbed their way to the shrub border at street level. Park Jobae and d grabbed at the branches of royal azaleas and scampered up as well, then jumped over the metal railing. They managed to find a side street near Supyo-gyo that wasn't blocked and make their way to Jongno. They reached the subway station at Jongno-3-ga. d realised they had come full circle back to Sewoon Market after clocking off two hours earlier.

At the Jongno-2-ga intersection, d and Park Jobae made their way towards the Bosingak bell pavilion. Jongno-2-ga was as tranquil and resplendent as on any other day. The tall buildings buttressed by snazzy outlets like Keumkang Shoes, Uniqlo, and Giordano, and the rows of jewellery wholesalers were all brightly lit and open for business. People sauntering out of bars to head home or to the next drinking hole left a sour whiff in the air, and music blared through the open doors of eateries promoting their spring specials. The smell of KFC hung in the air. The avenue was almost empty; here and there people who'd made it out of Cheonggyecheon walked towards Gwanghwamun in small groups. Police officers blew on their whistles as they diverted what few cars remained east towards Dongdaemun. d and Park Jobae walked among the inebriated, the enamoured, the enthused who'd doffed their winter coats to greet the arrival of spring. As they got closer to Bosingak the pavement grew quiet. Passing Jonggak, the two of them walked into the road. The pavements were lost behind rows of police buses or ranks of helmeted troops. d and Park Jobae continued up the emptied road and finally arrived at the Sejong-daero intersection.

They drew near and realised for the first time that the car wall had an additional layer behind it: this second wall had remained out of view on their earlier approach from Cheonggye Plaza. Sejong-daero, the boulevard running north to south was entirely bisected by a double layer of the bus barricade, meaning no one could access either direction, north or south. d saw that the wide central avenue in the heart of the city had been voided entirely of cars and people. A young woman and a man holding chrysanthemums were looking through a gap in the car wall for an opening that would lead them out to Gwanghwamun Square. d watched as they failed to find a way through and headed east, heels echoing, towards Jonggak. The intersection at Sejong-daero had morphed into an empty interspace between two walls. Motionless, entirely silent; it may as well have been a vacuum. There was an outburst from Cheonggye Plaza, where d and Park Jobae had passed through about forty minutes ago. Now what? d looked up at the statue of Admiral Yi Sun-sin that loomed behind the police buses. The voices of the people here will never reach beyond this interval, this vacuum, d thought. So this is revolution, Jobae my friend. We haven't circumvented anything; we followed the course determined by the barricades like a couple of meek sheep. And washed up here, like sediment. The revolution's already happened, d thought. This is it, isn't it? A revolution that precludes revolution, a revolution devised by the same people who put up these walls... The night air was bracingly cold.

104   dd's Umbrella

Park Jobae was quietly looking up at the Kyobo Building, his hands still in his pockets.

That's literally the number one building of this city, did you know that? he said. 1 Jongno of Jongnogu, Seoul.

9

When something out of the ordinary occurs.

Every time d recalled Park Jobae's words, they saw the milky white urn. The urn containing dd's ashes. More than a year had passed since d last laid eyes on it, but each time the urn seemed to rematerialise in d's hands. The warmth of it against their skin was excruciating and d had to close their eyes. To think that all of dd was contained in that small, unadorned vessel... d didn't need a gym bag. As for the out-of-the-ordinary event... Was it though? Outside of? Separate? Because if it was, surely it wouldn't be dragging on like this, relentlessly and with no end in sight. There were no signs or omens here, just the interminable ongoingness of *this*, day after day after day. Park Jobae had talked as if the world might end at any moment, but d had their doubts. Implode?

Why would it?

It would simply carry on. Gutted of beauty and honesty, life. Not even breaking... But simply persisting, barefaced and dull. The bus turned a corner and came to a halt. d got out and walked into a crumbling apartment complex. They stopped to buy some apples and strawberries. They were here to visit Yi Seung-geun and Goh Gyeongja. Yi Seung-geun had quit his wood shop three or four years ago due to gout. Now

106   dd's Umbrella

he lived off the rent money from a shabby house he owned in Bucheon. All trace of his life as a woodworker had been expunged from his home, and his wife Goh Gyeongja had sunk into a deep depression. Yi Seung-geun and Goh Gyeongja and d sat on the living room sofa, the fruit laid out on plates. Yi Seung-geun alternated between attempts at friendly engagement — d hadn't visited for close to a year — and abrupt frostiness as if there was no love lost between them. The tenants were falling behind on their payments, Yi Seung-geun said. Your ma and I are strapped for cash these days, he added, as if this were d's fault. Goh Gyeongja stared sullenly at the plate and ate the strawberries. d saw that she only had one slipper on. It was the soft indoor kind and had green stripes. d knew she'd developed a habit of late of eating her meals straight out of mixing bowls. She would hold a plastic bowl between her thighs under the floor table as if to keep the food — usually some combination of rice and pre-prepared side dishes thrown together — out of sight and lift spoonfuls directly to her mouth. d saw her do this one day and asked her about it. Why go to the trouble of setting the table for Pa and me, then insist on eating scrambled food out of a bagaji that you won't even lift off the floor? Goh Gyeongja seemed taken aback. This is the way I like to eat, she said, it's good, you should try it too. In fact, why don't we all eat like this? Then she added, as though in her own defence, Thinking about the old days.

What old days? d asked, and Goh Gyeongja looked at them as if to say, what a question. When I was a child, this is how I ate, she said. d had heard an anecdote or two over the years, enough to have a general idea of Goh Gyeongja's childhood, how she'd been forced to work as a live-in domestic at the home of some relatives. Her parents were war refugees from

Hwang 107

Hwanghae-do in the North, and after they settled in Gwanghwagun in Gyeonggi-do, they'd made a living doing odd jobs, as they had no marketable skills and no savings, had birthed a son and two daughters, and lost the older daughter to tuberculosis. Goh Gyeongja grew up as the youngest of two until she became the charge of relatives who ran a dry goods shop and promised to give her a higher education, but there was to be no schooling at all, let alone higher education, for the domestic help she effectively became in that house, where her meals consisted of scraps mixed with rice in a bagaji that she ate once the grown-ups and cousins had left the table.

d gazed at the strawberry tops Goh Gyeongja had placed along the edge of her plate and remembered what dd had said after hearing about Goh Gyeongja's childhood: Your grandparents said they'd had no choice, times were too hard, but they chose to leave your mother and not your uncle, their son, in the care of relatives. They blamed it on poverty, but essentially it was because she was a girl. They sent her instead of him to have one less mouth to feed and so she could support the family through her labour, and in their choice it's likely there wasn't a moment's hesitation or regret. Was it out of nostalgia? d wondered. But what part of that difficult childhood could she possibly be nostalgic about? There must be something about the past she missed that had made her revert to eating out of a mixing bowl, mimicking the food scraps she'd eaten as a child. What though? What was in her past and what wasn't in it? Well, her child self was there, of course, while her present self wasn't... Does Ma still eat out of a bagaji? d asked. Yi Seung-geun nodded. She eats well, her appetite's very good, was his reply.

108 dd's Umbrella

d got up to leave after three hours. Goh Gyeongja had fallen asleep on the sofa, but Yi Seung-geun came to see them off. d caught a whiff of urine coming from their father's trousers. The house generally reeked of the elderly couple's body waste. This wasn't the first time d had noticed their parents' commingled yet distinct odour permeating the place. They assumed their parents were not unaware of the smell and had wondered what it must be like for two people who felt no affection for each other to share a living space and endure each other's body odour. Preoccupied by this thought, d would sometimes lose the thread of the conversation they were having with their ma or pa. There was a built-in shoe cabinet in the doorway, a dark box whose strong funk filled the small space around it. d knew it was filled with a disorderly pile of flattened dress shoes and trainers and men's and women's sandals that no one wore. All in disarray and decaying by degrees. As were the lives of Yi Seung-geun and Goh Gyeongja. d had to wonder: Had dd lived and their shared life continued, would the two of them have also, eventually, inevitably, reached this juncture? It was a brutal thing to consider. A feeble, contemptible tableau. But how beautiful it would have been all the same, to weary of life alongside dd, to waste away to nothing amid the various objects they owned separately and together. But robbed of life as well as a physical form to disintegrate, dd never would be part of any such scene. As for me — the realisation dawned as d stood by the doorway and searched Yi Seung-geun's face — it will come: A life emptied of even apathy and disillusion, and stripped of all warmth. This is the face I will come to wear, and I will have to bear it alone...

d remained unmoving by the door until the motion sensor light switched off. Yi Seung-geun asked d why their beloved wasn't with them today.

Why indeed, d thought.

Why is my beloved not here with me?

d was about to reply that they didn't know, but the words wouldn't come. Their lips tensed and their jaw refused to open. It must look like I'm smiling, d thought. Ears pulled back, mouth taut, chin rigid, eyes narrowed: is this smiling? Whatever's happening with my face right now, all this uncomfortable crumpling, does this count as a smile? But what was there to smile about? Was Yi Seung-geun's question somehow funny? d felt a tickling in the pit of their stomach. Afraid they would burst into laughter, d clamped their lips together. I don't know, they could have answered. I don't know but in fact I do, I know exactly why, and that's why I can only tell you that I don't, they could have said. Why is my loved one not with me? Because they're too small. You, me, dd, we're all so small, a single jolt is all it takes to hurl us to the ground.

*

Around the middle of May, a rumour circulated that an older man had been found dead in the market. A man who, according to the stories, had been renting one of the units on the top floor, which saw far fewer visitors than the rest of the building as most of the units there stood empty or were used only as storage. The rumour was that he'd been living there for years, coming and going without anyone noticing, until one of the caretakers discovered him and carried out his dead, unclaimed body. It was said the man's family name was Yoon, and upon hearing this Yeo Sonyeo headed to the fifth-floor caretaker's office and asked for the man's first name, only to be told off for being a nuisance when they were so busy, and on

110   dd's Umbrella

the basis of some absurd and baseless false rumour, too, when the fact of the matter was that not a single person had ever died under such circumstances in this building.

When d came by the shop later that evening, Yeo Sonyeo was deep in thought, bearing down on his chair and staring at an amp. d chose an album from dd's stack and placed it on the turntable. They put their rucksack on the floor and sat down. They listened. Their joints and muscles clicked and popped, releasing the tension of a day's worth of heavy lifting and traipsing up and down stairs.

It had been raining all morning. The dust-darkened window was shut and beyond it, the lights of Jongno blurred by the unceasing rainfall. Yeo Sonyeo checked the circuit board with a test stylus. The fried parts were entirely unresponsive and the condenser beneath wasn't flowing very well either. All parts that were now obsolete, but Yeo Sonyeo had a few functioning replacements he'd collected from other devices. Holding a soldering iron, Yeo Sonyeo melted the leads around the burnt resistors. He removed what was dead and what was behaving suspiciously, put in the newer parts, soldered these into place. Lead smoke pooled above the worktable. Yeo Sonyeo opened the window. The hot and cool air mingled instantly. He tried to hoist the amp back up, but it was too heavy and there wasn't much space to manoeuvre on the table, so he asked d to give him a hand. d turned off the stereo and walked over. Together they raised the amp up by ninety degrees to lay it down right side up, then plugged in the vacuum tubes that had been set aside. When the power was switched back on, all five valves lit up with a soft, dim light. Yeo Sonyeo waited until the tubes had warmed up, then turned the radio dial at random. *Next up is Zion. T's 'Eat'... a former comedian has been detained for sexually assaulting a man in his twenties... Miwohaneun miwohaneun miwohaneun maeumeobsi Akkimeobsi akkimeobsi... two cases of Middle East Respiratory Syndrome have been confirmed in Korea for the first time... the Japanese girl group AKB48's Senbatsu General Election fever is sweeping the nation... a truck and taxi have collided on Gangbyeonbuk-ro leading to traffic hold-ups in both directions...*

Why are there bulbs inside amps? asked d.

Bulbs? Ah, these are vacuum tubes, not bulbs, Yeo Sonyeo said. Different structures, different roles. A bulb has nothing to do with sound, but a vacuum tube or valve determines the sound characteristic. Rectification and amplification, do you know what that means? Rectification gets what's scattered flowing in one direction and amplification increases the amplitude of a signal, and in an amp these tubes are what's responsible for doing that. Which is why they've got to be warmed up properly. The valves must be switched on properly for the amp to breathe, and for everything to flow properly.

Yeo Sonyeo stretched and yawned, saying the foul weather was making him feel all crumpled. Noticing how d seemed unable to tear away their eyes from the tubes, he asked if they'd like to have a listen and turned the dial to the cleanest channel he could find. d stood and listened to Brahms's 'Sapphische Ode' from Fünf Lieder, Op. 94.

Well, is it any different?

I can't tell.

Listen.

Well... maybe a little?

Yeah?

It does sound a little different, d said.

Yeah? It's different, is it? You can hear the difference?

112   dd's Umbrella

Prompted by Yeo Sonyeo's cheerful voice, d asked if this was a better-quality amp, but Yeo Sonyeo put his hands in his trouser pockets and said, Who knows.

Before TRs they had to add these tubes. Vacuum tubes are tricky to handle and liable to break, so when silicon was invented we got TRs. Pack TRs together and you have an IC, that's integrated circuits. So this here's a vintage machine, used before they invented TRs and ICs. These days the world moves so fast that even TR amps are considered vintage machines... But some people say TRs lack the romance of valve amps. Then there are those who prefer TRs because they have more power, and for the same reason others prefer these tube types to TRs. So you can't really say one is better than the other.

Yeo Sonyeo turned the dial again and they listened to Ella Fitzgerald sing 'Blue Moon'. d stared at the tube, unable to look away. Such a fragile object. Even in the sounds that had passed through these tubes there was a fair amount of noise. d peered at the vacuum inside the perilously thin glass shell and was reminded of the place where they'd lingered, with Park Jobae, a few days ago. *That* vacuum had been a spacious, dark, stilled suspension, whereas this small, unimportant vacuum was alive with light and signals. d thought again of the vacuum they'd sensed at the Sejong-daero intersection, of the erasure of flow from that space and of what lay beyond it, the people who'd gathered and had lingered there. Those people shared almost nothing in common with d. They had different experiences of life, of place, of death. They've lost their loved ones, I've lost my loved one. But those people had been fighting, resisting. What was it they were battling? Their smallness, of course, their smallness.

Why is my loved one not with me?

Do you feel a special connection to your sound system now? asked Yeo Sonyeo. No two audios are alike, you know, even if they're the same model, because the sound changes depending on the person handling it, he said. There's only ever one of it in the world, and that's why people don't say they're fixing a vintage device, they say they're reviving it.

A damp wind blew into the repair shop. Yeo Sonyeo closed the window against the splattering rain. Inside the scorched glass valve, a light glowed. d reached out unthinkingly and grabbed the limpid sphere. Searing heat. They pulled back at once.

Pain.

d stared at the valve in astonishment. The fiery temperature and frail thinness of the glass membrane were scored on their skin. The sting of the burn was like a thorn in their hand. Don't you underestimate it, Yeo Sonyeo said. Those tubes can get extremely hot, you have to watch out.

When it's time to go home, they'll each need an umbrella.
— 'Didi's Umbrella', from the collection *Pa ssi's Beginnings* (2012)

There Is Nothing that Needs to Be Said

1

It is past noon. Everybody's asleep. Which isn't surprising since we barely slept last night. There's something magical about this afternoon though. For everyone to be asleep at this hour, for it to be this quiet when we're all under one roof: what are the odds?

I put the cups and plates away and wipe the table. Once that's done, I'll move the books and laptop back. The table's in the living room. It's made of a bright brown wood that's moderately water-resistant. The legs are of exactly the right girth to support the square tabletop and this makes the table suitable for both eating and working, despite its somewhat malleable surface — a fork or ceramic plate placed on it with some force, even the corner of a book, is enough to dint it. It has its share of nicks and bruises, which only increase with time. Kim Sori says there's something brazen about this table and how easily it yields to pressure, not to mention how easily it accumulates dents, but I like to open a book or my laptop over these impressions. This is where I write. I try to work on my story whenever I have a spare moment. It's a story I've been meaning to finish.

I have eleven manuscripts that have yet to become short stories and one manuscript that has yet to become a novel.

120   dd's Umbrella

None of them are done. I've made a folder on my desktop for the drafts: twelve texts in all, each of them in progress. Perhaps it's more accurate to call them attempts, or the traces of attempts. With each attempt I've tried to tell the story. That one story.

A story in which no one dies.

Is it in me to write a story called 'The Finish Line'?

Why do you think your writing gravitates towards dead or good-as-dead people? I was asked once. This same person went on to say my stories would benefit from more heart. Writing advice from a group of readers online, a writing workshop if you will. Each of us paid a weekly fee of ₩10,000 to read and comment on each other's work. *Try to care more for your characters, i.e., people* — a comment I can't seem to forget. A lack of care: is that my problem? Is that why death features so prominently in my stories, and why they inevitably hit a wall?

I wonder how other writers manage to finish their stories. How do they know the story ends where it ends? I have a list of favourite books like everyone else, but the titles on my admittedly rather short list tend to be from the last century and were all written in longhand, with ink and paper. I've never written a story by hand. I've never even tried to, knowing how much paper I'd waste. If I had, would my output have been different? The laptop and pen are two entirely different implements, after all, and the tools we have at our disposal have a huge influence on what we say and think. When, as now, I sit at the table trying to write and find instead that my lips are dry as if from speaking at length, my thoughts return to handwriting. I think about Hauge's sheet of paper and Nietzsche's typewriter.

Olav H. Hauge, a gardener who struggled with schizophrenia, once wrote an ode to the fresh sheet of paper and fine cloth laid on his table in hopes that these would bring forth words.

New tablecloth, yellow!
And fresh white paper!
The words will come
for the cloth is good
And the paper fine!
When ice freezes over the fjord
birds come to settle

The paper and tablecloth that appear in Hauge's poem were most likely plain and ordinary. No connotations there, but simply: *New tablecloth! Fresh white paper!* I found the poem charming. I'm not partial to exclamation points, but I did find the ones here to be exceptionally endearing and felt a surge of kinship towards Hauge. Though in the very next page of the book he introduced a poetic narrator who pesters his wife Bodil to weave him a carpet, exclaiming that he means to wear the carpet around his shoulders each morning, and shouts for his breakfast table to be set, which unsettled me. One day Hauge would have approached the table — a table that could have been circular or square and may have been carried out into his garden or to a clearing in the woods — and he would have seen, with astonishment, the new tablecloth and blank page laid out on it. Reading Hauge's poem, I could see the paper in front of me. The blank white page, as inviting as a freshly cut loaf of bread, on which the poem 'New Tablecloth' would come to be written.

122   dd's Umbrella

I'm certain Hauge wrote this poem by hand. A pencil would have been just the thing. I like to imagine him scratching at a piece of paper with pencil lead. If he had fed the sheet into a typewriter to imprint it with metal type, he wouldn't have felt its delicate texture in quite the same way, so I imagine his hands were resting on the page as he wrote. After all, as quite a few of us know from experience, the surest way to appreciate the materiality of paper is by touching, tearing, folding, smelling, and scratching. It saddens me that I can't handle the reams of paper I own in quite the same way.

I collect paper in the form of books. The printed book seems a more complete form of bound paper than, say, the notebook. And I prefer volumes with illustrations and sentences over photos and images for how they feel against my hand. Often I'll buy books purely for the thickness or texture of their endpapers, the colour of the ink, or the quality of printing. Translated books like the first edition first printing of Jack Kerouac's *On the Road*, published 19 October, 2009, in Lee Mansik's translation, or the first printing of Eugene Dabit's *North Hotel*, published on 16 February, 2009, in Yu Gihwan's translation. That was how Hauge's book of poetry found its way into my hands too, and I find its materiality pleasing. There was a time when I used to purchase two copies of the same book for the quality of the paper alone. Though I stopped doing that when I realised no two books are alike, even if they are printed on the same day by the same printer and with the same ink. There are always subtle variances, whether in ink concentration or in print quality. For instance, on page 172 of the copy of Stefan Zweig's *The World of Yesterday* translated by Gwak Bokrock that I've just opened, there is a long passage on Rainer Maria Rilke, an explanatory passage that is more an ode to Rilke, that doesn't repeat in any other copy of this 2014 edition published by Jisik gongjakso. This passage is printed beautifully in clear black ink in my copy of *The World of Yesterday*, but the odds that the printing of this passage will be quite the same in other copies of *The World of Yesterday* are very slim. Their copies will be as distinct as other people's experiences of yesterday are distinct from mine. The title, author, translator, and publisher are all identical and in that sense this is only a minor discrepancy, but it is a discrepancy nonetheless and to some people a significant one. I have to say, all this makes me wonder if my fascination with paper has more to do with the materiality of black ink on paper... But to get back to my point, each copy of a book has a distinct smell as well. The pages I happen to own exude an odour that's similar to faded construction paper, but other pages will smell of other things. After all, every book takes on the scents of its surroundings.

Then there's Nietzsche. In 1882, as his eyesight deteriorated, Nietzsche purchased a Malling-Hansen typewriter, thanks to which he could carry on his work. Writing on a typewriter must have been a radically different experience from writing directly on paper with pen in hand. With a fountain pen you had to control the pressure every time the nib grazed paper, for one. I'm convinced Nietzsche would have experienced what bordered on awe as he made the conversion from handwriting to typewriting. The doctor Jacques Rogé, the philosopher Karl Jaspers, and academic Goh Byeong-gwon have all commented on Nietzsche's transformation around 1881 and attempted to identify what gave him such cheer, what mental leap he may have experienced to bring on such a drastic change in outlook.

124   dd's Umbrella

'What happened to him? What gave birth to the Will to Power, the Eternal Return, the Übermensch? What had he experienced prior to writing *Zarathustra*?', Goh Byeong-gwon asks in *Nietzsche's Dangerous Book: Thus Spoke Zarathustra* — but I would like to submit the typewriter for consideration here, to be included on the list of possible reasons. Nietzsche would have had to punch out each letter on his typewriter. A groundbreaking adaptation from the sustained application of pressure that strains bone and muscle to the instantaneous light strokes of the keys; from a delayed method of writing that could never match the speed of thought to an assembly that was speedier, its rhythms more resolute. A novel tool. It must have exerted a tremendous influence on Nietzsche's writing from the outset. As well as adding a musical element to the process. I wonder how he handled his typewriter. And the sentences that were born amid that transition, what time did they beat?

The keyboard I use isn't attached to a typewriter, that is to say I use a word processor, which is a different departure altogether from the earlier shift from handwriting to typing. One requires the handling of a finite or defined number of pages, the other scrolling through an unending stream of virtual paper. Individual pages smudged with transferred carbon on the one hand, anxiety-inducing screen pages that could potentially revert to zero from system failure, whether due to software or hardware issues on the other... Perhaps most significantly, the backspace keys function differently. On a typewriter the backspace key overlays the mistaken sentence with another, making a mess of the page, whereas on a word processor the key simply voids the earlier sentence, and there isn't a page to make a mess of in the first place.

If Nietzsche had owned a word processor, what would have become of his Übermensch? Some say speculating about history is pointless, but I enjoy woolgathering on occasion. Nietzsche, in his 1887 book *On the Genealogy of Morals*, didn't stop at naming one Übermensch but affirmed his own people as *gut* and called the Goths a 'godlike race' — 'one sees what in ancient Rome "the good" meant for a man. Must not our actual German word *gut* mean "the *godlike*, the man of godlike race"? and be identical with the national name (originally the nobles' name) of the *Goths*?' — but what if he'd foreseen in the future of that sentence the appearance of extermination camps? What then would he have done with those sentences? Would he have deleted them, spitting at people who read as convention dictated and only as they wanted to read, for being far from the 'perfect reader' he wished for? Would he have erased and emptied the page and started over? Considering how he was already well-versed in imagining the future, if he'd had a word-processing device at his disposal...

But enough of that.

I'd like to get started on my thirteenth story. Will I manage to finish it? What will I need to do so? Care: is that a tool that will serve me well? I don't recall who told me that quote, about how *people are bound to speak and think according to the tools they have at hand*, whether that be money, language, or smartphones...

My friend Y, who has a degree in arts education and used to be an ardent reader of Marx and Žižek and Geoff Eley's book *Forging Democracy: The History of the Left in Europe, 1850–2000*, made an abrupt volte-face in their midthirties. Abandoning the dream of a worker's world to come, Y converted to the

126 dd's Umbrella

religion of unearned income overnight and purchased a dilapidated multi-unit residential as a 'gap investment', for which they only needed to pay the difference after subtracting existing tenants' substantial jeonse rent deposits from the depreciated property price. The building was in such a state of disrepair that Y soon had permanent worry lines on their forehead and lived in fear of tenants demanding repairs and renovations.

One time Y was livid with a young couple for managing to break their boiler in under three months — a boiler that had been installed twenty-one years ago. Y griped that the new tenants must have abused the boiler for it to start malfunctioning after twenty years. Then there was the time Y had to pay for three paintings damaged by a leak. The artist tenant lived in the semi-basement, but water had seeped down from the top floor through the walls. When the tenant demanded compensation, Y went to look at the paintings, decided all they needed were new frames, and went so far as to visit an art supply store and fit the paintings in the frames themself. Y figured the paintings were as good as new now but the artist disagreed, and in the end, Y had to pay up. An amount that, as Y later calculated, was identical to the sum of the agent commission and moving fee for the artist, and Y had complained bitterly of the tactics of 'tenants these days'. Y was especially indignant since they were convinced the paintings would never find a buyer. They seemed to expect my commiseration, but my mind had drifted while they recounted their ordeal to the words echoing in my head: *people are bound to speak and think according to the tools they have at hand...*

But enough of that.

I'll have to wake everyone up soon. Seo Sookyung and Kim Sori and Jung Jinwon. The day's in full swing and we all have plans for the afternoon. But I won't wake them just yet. I sit at the table with the book open, chin in hand, and glance over at the living room window. The window is fitted with a single pane, which doesn't help with the heat or the cold. Two sheets of glass, murky with age, are fitted in the frames; they're unlikely to have been removed from the sill since they were first installed, back when this multistorey was put up. The frame is a deep purple. I don't know much about architectural aesthetics, but even I can tell that the colour of those frames isn't complementary to the rest of the building. Who chose that particular shade of purple?

Beyond the glass there are a couple of trees that partially block the view of the houses opposite, which I appreciate. I've no wish to look through other people's windows. It's mostly piles of clutter that meet your eyes anyway, objects stored away in glorified storage spaces we call balconies then forgotten about or stashed out of sight in hopes they won't have to be dealt with. But thinking about these rejected, neglected, forgotten objects glimpsed through glass reminds me of a certain landscape of common sense, and that's not something I like to dwell on. Fortunately, all I see out of this window are trees. A bird just flew past above their slender, still-bare branches.

How will this day be remembered?

Being five years old, Jung Jinwon is unlikely to remember its details for long. At most they'll retain fragments and impressions: the bread, the fried eggs, their ma sobbing, the adults' silence... Will Seo Sookyung and I still be together

128 dd's Umbrella

when Jung Jinwon is fully grown? How so? Will we be able to explain ourselves? Explain this day? That today was today?

At some later date I'll think back to the exact point when all these stories began. But where *is* the beginning? I was born, Seo Sookyung was born, Kim Sori was born, Jung Jinwon was born — is that what beginnings are? I was born at night. Or so I've been told by my pa, but are his tales credible? Do I credit them? There was a pear tree outside the ward, according to him. It was a difficult birth, and after looking in on the baby, he'd gone to get some air and there, at the entrance to the ward, happened to glance up and was met by the sight of fresh pear blossoms against the night sky. I don't believe in that night, but I do picture that scene from time to time. Were the pear blossoms still there on the morning of Seo Sookyung's birth? Would they have held on for the next nine nights? Seo Sookyung and I were born in the same labour ward of the same hospital in the same year, both in the third month of the lunar calendar. On the eighth day in my case, and Seo Sookyung on the seventeenth day. Could that be a way to begin?

2

Seo Sookyung spent most of her childhood within the confines of Gonghangdong in Gangseogu, Seoul's airport neighbourhood, where she grew up watching aeroplanes. There was a low hill, she said. Uninterested in sedentary activities, Seo Sookyung was always running from one place to another, with or without purpose or destination. Running was her idea of fun. When she grew tired she'd climb the bare shadeless hill and stare up at the sky until a plane passed over her. From where she lay she could see the entire underbelly of the hulking machines as they rose over the hill, swallowing up the surrounding air and sounds behind them. The undercarriages would be out and Seo Sookyung could make out the screws in the wheel well. The proximity of those machines meant she never imagined a future for herself that didn't involve laying her hands on them.

Straight out of high school she enrolled in college to study aerospace engineering. This fact always gives me pause — that Seo Sookyung had such a clear and specific vision of her future at that young age — as it's not an experience I or Kim Sori share. Having grown up with parents who had bad credit for a long time, Kim Sori and I were conscious of our poverty and predicament, but what we should therefore do, what we could

130   dd's Umbrella

do, or what we might become were not something either of us imagined in any detail. The two of us were, much like our parents, frequently despondent and habitually despairing, and the fact that the future would nonetheless come knocking and that we might do something to meet that future had seemed inconceivable. Kim Sori was unlike me and worked various part-time jobs, but these only ever covered immediate necessities; at no point had she envisaged the future or expected or even hoped for a better one, as she later told me. Whenever she found us sunk in despair or paralysed by self-pity, Seo Sookyung helped us grasp the situation for what it was and encouraged us to move and act in the moment to prepare for whatever was coming next. Seo Sookyung's ability to imagine the future undoubtedly made her who she is, at least for a period of time. And that version of Seo Sookyung was what inspired me and Kim Sori precisely where we had most needed inspiration: in our daily lives.

Seo Sookyung and I may have been born in the same ward of the same hospital and grown up in the same district, but having attended different primary, middle, and high schools, we had almost no point of contact growing up. From middle school on however we did have occasion to see each other once a year, first at the yearly preliminary rounds of the National Junior Athletics Championships and then at the National Athletics Championships for High School Students. We represented our schools in the preliminary rounds that would determine the regional teams. Seo Sookyung ran the sprint and long-distance, I was in relays and throwing. As my school lacked athletes, the PE teacher had randomly assigned those events to me. In our district not many schools had a proper athletics team or a coach. Most of us competing in sprints, long distance, relays, long jump, discus, and javelin had been selected through a process whereby a teacher would hand a javelin or a discus and say, Here, give this a go, or You, throw this; or draw a line in the sand and say, Jump from there to here — then tell us all we had to do was show up at the appointed place and time and simply run, throw, hurl, or jump as we'd just done. And we did as we were told; we showed up. The teachers who chaperoned were mostly PE teachers who had no experience as coaches. Their inexperience was such that they would order jajangmyeon and jjamppong for us on the day of the long-distance runs. These floury, greasy dishes sat heavy on our stomachs, and the runners would turn blue in the face as they lagged behind. But mostly the teachers didn't care, they were only going through the motions. Once the events were underway, they would stand around in the shade, hands behind their backs, making small talk, or disappear off somewhere and come back with soju on their breath. We received no training to speak of, and simply ran or jumped or threw in whichever field the preliminary round happened to be taking place. Every year the same kids would show up, and with each passing year we began to notice how much we'd grown and what physical changes we were each undergoing.

Seo Sookyung was one of the few athletes who always performed well at these meets. Through middle and high school she still came in first in most of the events, although she ran on behalf of schools that didn't have an athletics team or a proper training regimen. When Seo Sookyung ran, the teachers and athletes would crowd around to see her. I once heard someone say that there was something in the way she

132   dd's Umbrella

ran, but I felt a more accurate observation would be that there was an *absence* of something in the way she ran. When she ran, she ran. Without ambition, worries, rivalry, or even an eye towards the finish line or the record, and without superfluous movements or personal mannerisms. She ran in the most minimal way, with only the necessary movements, so that in her running I could see, as in a passage I later came across in Saint-Exupéry's *Wind, Sand and Stars,* something akin to how 'the curve of a piece of furniture, or a ship's keel, or the fuselage of an aeroplane' has 'no longer anything to take away' rather than having 'no longer anything to add'.

The first time I saw Seo Sookyung, she was running. I was sipping a Del Monte juice box, waiting for the boys' long-distance race to end. We had no ice boxes, let alone cold storage, and the crates of lukewarm, overly sweet flavoured drinks did nothing to quench my thirst. The boys had entered their last lap and were headed for the finish line. Suddenly, out of nowhere, a light-footed runner in white jersey shorts and matching shirt dashed past me at great speed.

Pat-pat-pat-pat.

Seo Sookyung hates it when I describe her running like this, but that was what I heard as she sped around the track and quickly grew distant. At first I thought it must be the last runner in the boys' long-distance event, but it turned out to be Seo Sookyung, leading in the girls' group. Seo Sookyung was ahead by half a lap when a handful of girls ran past me in a cloud of dust. That's how fast she was. I was pretty clueless about sports and athletics back then, but I still knew, almost instinctively, that I was witnessing raw talent on its path to prominence. That girl's going to be famous, I thought. With that much speed and presence, she's on her way to becoming someone great.

But the year we both turned seventeen, Seo Sookyung stopped coming to the meets. Her knees were ruined, thanks to her PE teacher's deleterious combination of incompetence and greed. Fired up by Seo Sookyung's impeccable record, the teacher had sent her to any and all meets and competitions and trained her, but the training had no basis on theory or study and was closer to boot camp drills or physical punishment. Seo Sookyung had to undergo knee surgery, after which she was never able to run as she once did. But all Seo Sookyung had to say about that was: I wasn't really into sports anyway. After a competition the teachers would always ply the athletes with sweet and sour pork or egg fried rice, and this, she claimed, was the only reason she'd run in the first place. From time to time she did imply in passing that her life might have turned out differently had she received proper training, and I'd think about how Seo Sookyung was the third daughter of five children, four girls and a boy. Parents and money are, to a large degree, what make or break junior athletes, and Seo Sookyung never could depend on one or the other.

Seo Sookyung concentrated on her academic work for what remained of high school and was accepted to study aerospace engineering at university, where through a combination of scholarships, student loans, and endless part-time jobs, she eventually obtained her degree. Once, after wondering about the study of aerospace engineering, I'd asked Seo Sookyung, Why do they call it *aerospace*? Aren't air and space distinct domains set apart by the presence or absence of gravity and

134   dd's Umbrella

atmosphere? We were sitting at a Lotteria eating french fries and Seo Sookyung, who had been sipping on her straw, raised her eyes at me and said that by definition a body had to pass through Earth's atmosphere in order to enter space from Earth, meaning it first had to undergo drag and gravity.

But these conversations came later, after my second encounter with Seo Sookyung. Back in high school, not knowing what had become of her, I assumed she must be attending other district or regional preliminaries. The more outstanding athletes were often approached by teacher scouts who coaxed them into switching schools and hence districts, to a school with a proper athletics team, and I assumed that was what had happened to Seo Sookyung. I was certain that wherever she was, she would still be running. I was so certain of this that I followed the news with interest any time there was a national competition, but somehow, I never came across her name.

It was on the Yonsei University campus that I ran into Seo Sookyung again, during the 6th August 15 Grand Reunification Festival cohosted by Jochongnyon, North Korea's National Alliance of Youth and Students for National Reunification, and Hanchongnyon, the South Korean Federation of University Students Councils.

3

I entered university in 1996, after re-sitting my college entrance exams. This made Seo Sookyung my senior. I was a member of the Seoul East Regional Branch of the Seoul Regional Federation of University Students Councils and she a member of the Incheon-Bucheon Regional Branch of the Gyeonggi-Incheon Regional Federation of University Student Councils, and we each found ourselves trapped in Jonghap Hall at Yonsei University for several days in August 1996. After attempting to find a route out of the besieged campus and pursued by combat police, thousands of us had escaped into Jonghap Hall and barricaded ourselves, only to be stranded there. We were isolated for several days at most, but what I experienced during those few days would frame my impression of the entire year. I still have flashbacks at the mere mention of 1996, despite the intervening years and the multitude of other incidents and crises since. Yonsei 1996 remains lodged in my throat, a bodily, sensory memory: the pepper fog, the smell of liquid tear gas dropping from the sky like smir, the hunger and the thirst, the terror of night raids and arrests, the back of a classmate festering from the heat, humidity, and exposure to chemical agents, the palpable state and stench of other people's skin, the overwhelming desire to wash my face and brush my

136   dd's Umbrella

teeth, the *How'd you wash your cunts, you filthy slags.* ('During the nine days Yonsei University was under siege, the police denied students access to food, medical supplies, and even feminine hygiene products. [...] they also denied the occurrence on August 20 of unacceptable instances of sexual assault and violence towards female students when they entered the campus and dragged students away for interrogation. [...] As they hauled female students out of the building, police ordered them to bend over and grab the waist of the person ahead to form a train. Once the female students complied, they proceeded to fondle their chests and hips [...] "It's always the ugly ones who get swept up in protests. Protesting 'cause no one will give them the time of day. That's what it is, right? 'Cause the boys won't give you the time of day? Hey. How'd you wash your XXX [explicitly referring to female genitals] anyway? Filthy slags. You haven't washed for ten whole days, have you? I can smell your female parts. So how many times did you put out? Come on, we know you did, to thank the guys on the frontline, right? You XXXs."' Goh Sangman, 'Why Choo Mi-ae, Newly Elected Member of the National Assembly, Recited Obscenities during the Annual Government Audit', *OhmyNews*, 29 Aug, 2016.)

The August heat was sweltering, the air muggy after several days of rain. The authorities had cut the building's water and electricity supply and a helicopter hovered overhead spraying tear gas throughout the day. We couldn't open the windows as tear gas coated the outer walls, and the hall was a furnace to which night brought no relief. After days of going without food or water, we started to sweat less, which was one comfort at least — sometimes we would unthinkingly wipe the sweat from our brows, only to have tear gas enter our eyes and suffer the consequences. On the day the police made their way into the hall for the last time, we were pushed onto the rooftop by the cops and the flames up to the rooftop and arrested well

Hwang 137

before noon. Then feeling more starved, exhausted, and lethargic than we'd ever been in our lives, we were made to file down the ash- and lye-heaped stairs with our hands on the shoulders of the person in front of us and squat on the cement ground outside the building. I was squatting as ordered with my head on my knees, secretly relieved, as everyone else was, that at least the isolation part was over, when I realised I'd been staring blankly at a face in profile. A face I recognised. It was Seo Sookyung. Wearing a green and ivory striped T-shirt and dark cotton trousers, she sat hugging her calves, her face peeking out from atop her knees, wet trainers on bare feet. She gazed ahead at nothing in particular — I noticed her lips were torn — then bowed her head. Her right chin and neck were marked with soot, probably from touching the scorched wall on her way down from the roof.

Recognising her, the very first words I said to her were: I know you.

I told her my name, listed when and where and at which competitions our paths had crossed, but Seo Sookyung remained impassive. Yeah, nice to see you, was all she had to say, her face and eyes revealing nothing. It was as if her whole countenance were enveloped in a thin but tough membrane, and despite her words she didn't seem glad or pleasantly surprised to see me. I on the other hand was happy at the reencounter. In that brief interval, so brief it felt like the blink of an eye, I spoke of how we'd both been in the Junior Athletic Championships and asked if she was studying PE now at uni. No, she replied, she was studying aerospace engineering. Do you have a beeper?, *I do*, Give me your number, *Here you go* — so the conversation went, at warp speed by my standards, both then and now, before we were led away. We were each assigned

138 dd's Umbrella

stations, interviewed by the police, categorised as simple participants, cautioned, and sent home. I got in touch not long afterwards, and we spoke over the phone every chance we got, conversations that lasted well into the night — and when we met up it was hard to part again for all we had to discuss, we talked about everything and anything and would wind up sitting in a park until dawn, waiting to see the sunrise. It didn't take very long for us to figure out that what we needed most was a place where we could be together. As of this year, Seo Sookyung and I have been living together for twenty years.

The first few times I contacted Seo Sookyung, I found her somewhat curt and monosyllabic, as I had in our previous exchange, and noticed a general disinterestedness or aloofness. But as it turned out she was a surprisingly reliable interlocutor.

She was on campus that day because of her role as interim secretary of the Engineering College Student Council. The actual secretary, overcome by lethargy and a general malaise, had abruptly stopped attending meetings earlier that year, and the council president, concerned about the management of union funds, had pleaded with Seo Sookyung to take on the role. She'd accepted on the condition that it would be temporary. Seo Sookyung remembers the nostalgic refrain that circulated like some legend at her university back then: *We are the true militant activists, the toughest in our region, the truly hardcore protestors…* But as far as Seo Sookyung could see and hear and sense, it was pure spin, one of those lingering tall tales that every university boasts, like permanent snow in a landscape painting on the wall. In 1995, the year Seo Sookyung entered uni, the atmosphere on college campuses was already far removed from the days of mass demonstrations. What's there to

Hwang   139

protest, there's nothing *to* protest under a civilian government, was the general sentiment, and student councils shifted their focus to issues of student welfare like freezing school bus fares or improving the cafeteria menu. And given that her position was temporary, Seo Sookyung didn't feel particularly bound to either the University Student Council or to Hanchongnyon.

The main reason Seo Sookyung attended the Pan-National Rally and the Grand Reunification Festival of 1996 as a council representative was because of the death of Noh Soo-seok in March of that year. (Noh Soo-seok was born on 23 November, 1976, in Gwangju, entered Yonsei University College of Law in 1995, and died on 29 March, 1996, as a consequence of police kettling and suppression during the Seoul Regional Federation of University Student Council's Rally to Demand President Kim Young-sam's Campaign Finance Disclosure and to Secure Education Funding. Noh Soo-seok was recognised as a participant of the pro-democracy movement by the Committee for Democratic Movements Activists' Honor Restoration and Compensation on 9 September, 2003. Source: Noh Soo-seok Memorial Society website.) Noh Soo-seok died while being pursued by combat police near Euljiro in central Seoul, an area Seo Sookyung had frequented since middle school for its cinemas and fast-food chains. Seo Sookyung was shocked that someone could die at the hands of the police in streets she knew like the back of her hand, and the fact that Noh Soo-seok was her age came as another blow. When she saw the notices for the rally at Yonsei in August, her first thought was of her fellow twenty-year-old, the Yonsei College of Law student who met his death during a protest. She told me she felt indebted.

But that had been the extent of it. She hadn't felt compelled to take part in the struggle; pan-nationalism and reunification

140   dd's Umbrella

were of no interest to her. In the months and years that followed, she was to regret this. One of the juniors Seo Sookyung had gone to Yonsei with that day in 1996 was hauled into police custody for throwing stones at the plainclothes police force known as Baekgoldan, the White Skull Corps, due to their white helmets and gas masks. Another friend, struck by the zeal of the Gwangju-Jeonnam Regional Federation of Student Councils, later known as the Southern Federation of Student Councils or Namchongnyon, upon witnessing the President of Hanchongnyon, a Jeonnam University alumnus, shave his head in protest, had shaved his own head and joined the cause, and would leave uni without completing his studies. Seo Sookyung was haunted by the fact that she was the one who brought them there that day. Not with a particular resolve or intent or even much thought, but as casually as if they were going on a field trip, and she regretted having made light of the situation.

Seo Sookyung told me about one of the student council members, mentioning her by name. L was a mechanical engineering student in the entering class of '96, who, after the events of August 1996, periodically and over the course of several months failed to attend classes for about three days every month... An absence that coincided with her menstruation cycle. Gossip circulated about L's regular nonattendance and how it was due to her 'abnormal' PMS. No one recognised its relation to trauma. Trauma, Seo Sookyung repeated, and fell silent. I didn't know to think of it in terms of trauma either, not until much later, she continued. At the time I simply thought L was being too sensitive and that she hadn't quite come to terms with the experiences of that week. Later I began to see her sensitivity as eccentric. After all, we'd all been there, all gone through the same ordeal... and there wasn't much else we could do in the situation, was there? I suppose I thought having spent a few days with blood stains on our trousers wasn't that shameful, given the circumstances. I doubt L ever got a chance to speak to someone about it. None of us *could* talk about it. It was too distressing to remember let alone discuss, and besides, we thought it didn't warrant speaking about as we'd all been there; we assumed it didn't need to be said because we knew.

Seo Sookyung's term as interim secretary of the college student council continued until the end of the academic year when the council was dissolved, at which point Seo Sookyung cut ties with the council and focused on her studies. *First tend to your own front yard* became her mantra, but what she didn't know was that a whirlwind by the name of the IMF Crisis was headed straight for those front yards. With the financial crisis of 1997, seniors, juniors, and students from the same entering class began to vanish from campus, some on indefinite leave and others dropping out. Seo Sookyung managed to complete her degree by mustering all the student loans and labour and luck she could, only to discover on graduation that no one was hiring. She enrolled for a master's degree after a professor suggested she come and work in his research office, which would help her pay off her student loans while gaining research experience. His office researched and developed aircraft and combat flight simulations, and Seo Sookyung's job there was mostly administrative: keeping receipts for expenses, drafting and submitting project plans for academia and industry collaborations, contacting the accounting department of the simulator manufacturer, marking undergraduates' exam papers.

142   dd's Umbrella

In short, everything unrelated to research fell to her. While the men students gathered experimental data, Seo Sookyung would sit glueing meal receipts to paper and wondering whether the receipt for the professor's dental treatment could be filed under the office's welfare or reserve funds. The research office was located at room 1014, Gonghak Hall and shared by two Engineering professors. On the other side of the partition sat another master's student, Jiyoung, also in charge of receipts and paperwork, also the only woman.

What finally forced Seo Sookyung to give up her degree and walk out of that office was the scandalous chain of events around C's dissertation. C was a senior creating a simulation program that would be interoperable with helicopter simulators. The simulation experiments were part of a government-funded academia and industry collaboration, a project that came about via a contract with the defence industry company that manufactured the simulators. C's master's dissertation was based on these experiments, but since the experimental value was set beforehand and the simulation experiments were conducted so as to confirm this value, the quality of the dissertation was poor, to put it mildly. In his dissertation defence, the simulator that was interoperable with C's program either failed to operate or malfunctioned, and C was not only visibly flustered and unable to answer the questions posed by the department professors — How did you come up with these numbers? — but he ended up sobbing in front of his so-called experimental results. He was, Seo Sookyung told me, nonetheless awarded his degree on the basis of that dissertation. His dissertation advisor paid the other department professors a visit and explained how C was the 'head' of his household, having married his partner when she fell pregnant midway through his degree, and the professors were persuaded into agreeing that if C made a few adjustments to his dissertation they would award him his degree. When a bright-faced, carefree C handed a signed copy of his dissertation to her, Seo Sookyung found herself gawking at him, unable to take her eyes off his face. C's dissertation would help no one, in fact, given all its inaccuracies, it was more likely to cause harm to future researchers. Regardless, it would take its spot in the university library, its faulty contents obscured behind a laminated, dark blue, casebound physical exterior. As she was handed that glossy hardback, she said it was as if her mind cleared and what had seemed so complicated at once became simple, and she knew that she could not remain there a moment longer.

*

I enrolled in a Language and Literature Department of a certain university in 1996, only to quit the following year. Both decisions were made on a whim. I took the entrance exam as the unquestioned next step upon graduating from an academic high school with good marks. I had no other goals or interests so I headed to uni, and when I failed to find a motivation to stay, I left. Can the impossible be a motive? Because as soon the first term began, I knew I could not, would not, finish my studies. Whereas my peers considered it a matter of course to spend a period studying abroad or attending language courses in countries where their chosen languages were spoken and made concrete plans to that end from the first year, I'd struggled to scrape together the tuition fee as it was and could hardly see beyond the next two terms. Then there was the matter of the course lectures themselves.

144 dd's Umbrella

They were closer to beginner-level language classes than university lectures, and we were made to endlessly recite the subjective, objective, and possessive personal pronouns. Plus the pages of the textbooks were much too glossy and stiff and I was reluctant to put my hands on them. I drifted away from my lectures and department and spent most of my time in and around the student union building. I had joined the university pungmul band and skipped classes to play the buk and the janggu. Its members were devoted to revealing corruption within the university foundation and taking a political stance against the ruling party, but I didn't share their stance or their values. I liked instruments — that was the only reason I frequented the band room.

Aside from the drumming, my university life was as tepid as fog on a summer's morning. Like the early morning fog on campus one day, when I found myself sitting on a bench with my bandmate J. We'd been drinking all night in the band room and had crept outside at some point to escape the sour and mouldy funk and to breathe the cool morning air. But it was warm out and there was barely any breeze; a heavy fog was drawn around us, reaching almost to my knees. I listened as J droned on about his various affairs, leaning his head on my shoulder. Women keep dying because of me, he said. Two women fought over me and killed themselves and I'm so torn up about that right now, it's going to haunt me for the rest of my life. Then he mentioned Mishima Yukio, the artist he most adored and revered. I could tell from the way he spoke that J was not only intrigued by but possibly enamoured of the writer, by how Mishima had no qualms about publicly insulting fellow novelist Dazai Osamu for his supposed ugliness, and by his decision to end his life by disembowelment as he had written about in his fiction. J said he judged Mishima Yukio's life very highly in terms of aesthetics, for the man's devotion to and pursuit of beauty that led him to imitate literature in life and, ultimately, in death. I, on the other hand, was distracted by the smell of entrails. As a child, I'd had to walk past an open market on my way to and from school, and the tiny back street in the final stretch had been lined with stalls selling 'rejuvenating' meat. Walking past that street every day and inhaling the smell of chicken and dog meat, I came to know the particular stench that the entrails of an omnivorous body gives off. I doubt Mishima Yukio would have found *that* pleasant, I thought but did not say. Instead I sat feeling unsettled and acutely aware of J's head and the strange angle at which it lay on my shoulder and over my clothes, in part because my clothes were sticking uncomfortably to my skin. J was taller and slimmer than I was and had a longer waist, so why sit in this undoubtedly awkward and extremely uncomfortable manner? What was the reason? Did he want to ask me out? Was that why he was 'confessing' to the devastation he had wrought, to underscore his own charm that had led to *deaths*, was that why he wouldn't move his head? Not that I would ever agree to go out on a date with him if he did ask, as I was put off by his stuffy jacket with its padded shoulders and... But enough of that.

This is all to say that how I wound up at the rally and the Yonsei campus in 1996 wasn't that different from how Seo Sookyung wound up there. I had hung about, listless as fog on a summer morning, until I happened to find myself there that day.

Following August 1996, Hanchongnyon was declared a subversive organisation, the chairperson was hunted down and

146   dd's Umbrella

imprisoned, and the student body's aversion to activism, especially at Yonsei, grew to irreparable levels alongside worsening general sentiment towards protests and actions. The people who made it out of Yonsei that August returned home feeling ashamed and helpless that their very last slogan while they were still surrounded by the police had been *I want to go home*. They trudged home, scrubbed their faces and their teeth, gazed at their own haggard reflections, and headed to bed. On the next day, they returned to campus and to their classes, the idea of first tending to one's own yard clasped to their chests like some epiphany — only to be met by the massive tides of the IMF bailout, which swept them straight back out of the university gates, sometimes for good... while those who remained kept their heads down and tended to their own front yards. Still others found reasons to go on fighting a government that had not only declared its own people enemies of the state but had brutally suppressed them, though these were relatively few in number, and those ready to sympathise with their story were even fewer.

Seo Sookyung and I never spoke much about our isolation in 1996. We didn't discuss what we'd witnessed and felt while we were trapped in that building. The memory of that blockade remained buried, if unforgotten, for a long time. That is until 10 June, 2008, when the barricade of shipping containers appeared across the main boulevard in Gwanghwamun, and 20 January, 2009, when the Namildang Building in Yongsan, where local residents had been protesting redevelopment, was raided by police and erupted into flames. On both these occasions, that earlier experience came rushing back in all its specificity.

The wall of stacked shipping containers that blocked off the central boulevard of Gwanghwamun in June 2008 was slick with oil, a deterrent in case any protestors thought to climb over it. The moment it appeared, it was immediately dubbed Myung-bak Fortress and ridiculed, but having witnessed the evolution of barricades over time, Seo Sookyung and I were unable to laugh along. On the heels of Myung-bak Fortress, different forms of vehicles-as-barricade began to be employed and were fine-tuned to a level of sophistication at breakneck speed. But the germ of all this development, according to Seo Sookyung, likely lay in 1996, in what they'd learned corralling student activists that year. That 1996 had served as inspiration to the regime was something she was unable to cast from her mind for a very long time. The officials had realised something from the decline in student activism in the 1990s, she said. The public's aversion to demonstrators, for one. During the Yonsei University incident, state authority and activists alike had witnessed the public's contempt for 'violent' protestors, and the authorities would have observed this phenomenon with interest. People were shocked when the excavator blasted through the heavy iron gates of the university on 15 August, and though they knew it was the government's doing, they still condemned the protestors for their 'aggression'.

So then of course somebody high up must have observed all this and thought, Eureka, right? Seo Sookyung continued. Isolate them physically, then frame them with violence. A perfect and failproof discovery of the means. Physical containment alongside ideological containment, the severing of movement, of action from life. Or perhaps... removing the skin of the political from the everyday. In any case, the car wall would accomplish this. But a car wall is, well, as a barrier it is

148   dd's Umbrella

mobilised in riot control, but the moment people lay hands on it and rock it back and forth, it stops being a barrier and becomes the property of the state. The protestors' actions are now acts of property damage, not attempts to clear a path through a blocked road. The officials are happy. Officiating has just become easier. Kettle the crowd, trap them and restrict their movement. Then disseminate footage and images of the aftermath: the breached car wall, the shards of broken glass, the havoc wreaked by these miscreants. The public's sympathies will shift in favour of the officials. Scenes of property damage are extremely effective in achieving that end, Seo Sookyung went on. They can carry much more impact than scenes that show loss of life or the maiming of life. Why? Because it's easier to empathise with the former. The why of that is difficult to explain, but here and now that's what's easier, and things generally tend to move in the direction of what's easier. And what could easily happen very often does in this place.

Yes, I thought. *People are bound to speak and think according to the tools they have at hand.* And for some unfathomable reason, they do this even when their hands are empty...

4

In the summer of 1997, I made my way out of a vineyard in Gimpo and out of uni for good. I was in Gimpo with members of my pungmul band on volunteer farm work our college council had organised. When I walked away, I was wearing a T-shirt with the words AUGUST 15 DASH printed across its front, baggy trousers that tightened at the waist and around the calves with elastic cords, and a straw hat.

Earlier that day, I had been standing with the others in the village foreperson's front yard, waiting to be assigned the day's potato or cucumber patch or vineyard, when B, who was my age but my senior by a year in the band, angled his head towards my left shoulder to whisper an order to remove my jewellery. Hours later, I was still grappling with this fact as I worked the vineyard. Take that off at once, B had hissed in my ear. Didn't I know what a bad impression my jewellery would make on the 'poor' farmers, how indulgent and vain I'd come across? He warned me that this would only worsen the general negativity towards college students following the incident at Yonsei. We could all be denounced for what I had on my ears and around my neck. He went on: Do you know how hard it was for the council and for us, your sonbaes, to find a district after what happened at Yonsei last year? The farmers were

150   dd's Umbrella

reluctant to have us, they wanted to know what business college students had going up to North Korea and waving their university flags, they asked if that didn't make us all commie Reds and it was really, really tough to convince them otherwise, and now thanks to you we could all end up looking bad.

I had been assigned to a small vineyard where I planned to work alone all morning and afternoon. This particular vineyard wrapped pesticide-coated paper envelopes around their grapes. I had to blow into the envelopes to open them up, which meant I was breathing in the chemicals as I worked, and before long I was feeling a bit drunk. My throat was stiff and my chest tight. I worked in a crouch over the furrows, blowing and wrapping before shuffling on to the next bunch of grapes, and when I finally stood up, I felt lightheaded. I reached in my pocket to fish out the jewellery that had been poking at my thigh as I worked, and examined them. What were these grievously irreverent objects that threatened to thwart and undermine us all? They were a pendant necklace engraved with Saint-Exupéry's Little Prince, and a pair of ring earrings, barely one centimetre in diameter. Standing there with my palm open, I saw a bus approach in a cloud of dust. The bus came closer, stopped briefly, then left without picking anyone up. I walked through the furrowed vineyard, pushing the swordlike spikes of plantain weeds aside with my knees and feet, and once I'd made my way out of the field, stood at the signless bus stop and waited in the heat, climbed on the next bus that pulled up, and made my way back to Seoul.

I lost touch with the people at uni after that day, but now I find myself wondering what might have become of them. I write down the names I remember on a slip of paper. B and T and R and N... How are they? I wonder. What do they look like now? How do they live? Could I have passed one of them in the street in the last few months? My same-age sonbaes. B, as the sangsoe or lead, had always played the small gong, and liked to replicate the single-file gilnori walk if there were any juniors present, even when we weren't playing music. B led the way and the other players or, as in this case, subordinates, followed. B wouldn't allow a hubae to walk ahead of him. And when we went for drinks and ordered a single plate of tteokbokki or a pot of altang as anju, as we were all broke and that was all we could afford, B would suddenly yell out, in the middle of his spiel about the Seoul East Regional Branch of Seochongnyon, and about woori, minjok, minju — we, people, democracy: I forbid anyone who doesn't know how to hold their liquor from hogging the anju! Quit it, you bastards, we've barely enough as it is!

Another sonbae, T, was nicknamed 'fifth male heir, third eldest son'. Why? Because this was his mantra, everything he said was punctuated by this phrase. Not surprisingly, he himself embraced the nickname. He talked constantly about his status as the fifth sole male heir running in his family *and* the eldest son of two eldest sons before him, and how this meant that any woman who bore his son would receive a hundred million won, no questions asked — then he'd try to pin women students who were drinking next to him to the ground, or suddenly blurt out that he was horny while walking with them past this or that remote corner of the campus. People called him a nut job, but none of the seniors tried to put an end to these behaviours, and whenever we went for drinks or on group trips, anyone who was the same hakbeon as him or his junior, regardless of whether they were women or men, were

152   dd's Umbrella

only allowed to call on him by clapping their hands and shouting out the nickname. *Clap* FIFTH MALE HEIR *clap* THIRD ELDEST SON. We didn't find this particularly awkward, in fact we all joined in, following the rhythm, and some even laughed. Like it was a big joke. But I always despised T and never wanted to end up in the shitty, unfortunate, and potentially distressing situation of being alone with him, and I remember thinking that he was bound to get his comeuppance one day by being involved in a major sex scandal.

But as it turns out, he's just peachy. A few years ago I happened to see him out and about in Jongno, ranting at Lee Myung-bak's remarks about how unattractive women provide better service — ('The Grand National Party presidential candidate Lee Myung-bak, during a dinner on 28 August at a Chinese restaurant in the centre of Seoul with a dozen chief editors of the major national daily newspapers, is reported to have made improper analogies regarding "women" [...] At this dinner, which took place a week after his nomination by the Grand National Party, presidential candidate Lee Myung-bak is said to have discussed best ways for men to select women employed in "the special service industry" as part of the "life wisdom" he was imparting. [...] According to a chief editor present at the dinner, "Candidate Lee was imparting life wisdom and sharing stories about how he avoided military service and what he experienced of corporate life while working at Hyundai when he made the problematic statement." This editor went on to say, "Reminiscing about the years he worked overseas for Hyundai Construction, Candidate Lee made remarks along the lines of how 'The sonbaes who had been stationed there the longest told me that when they went to places with massage girls they chose the women who were less good-looking. I thought about why that might be, and it's because women with looks are likely to have had more men... [partly omitted by the editor] but the women who weren't as pretty gave better service… [partly omitted by the editor]'. This happened a fortnight ago so I won't say this is verbatim, but as I remember this was the gist of what he said"', Elections special coverage team, 'Presidential Candidate Lee Myung-bak Makes Improper Comparison to Newspaper Chief Editors, Says to Choose "Ugly Women" over "Good-looking Women"?', *OhmyNews*, 12 Sep, 2007.) — because, as he claimed, it's the good-looking ones that are also good in the sack.

In the summer of 1997, I made my way out of a vineyard and out of that place for good.

This is the opening line of a story I started writing about three or four years back, though I didn't get very far. The idea was to write about people fleeing a world laid waste, but try as I might, the story and the words all rang false. How could I write something I had a hard time believing? I wondered if the issue was that I had never experienced escape, a breaking free. I consulted Seo Sookyung, who asked if my leaving the vineyard in 1997 didn't count as one. Did it? For so long I'd told myself I'd run away from Gimpo that summer.

Had I run away, or had I broken free?

Are the two distinguishable?

One way or another, today passes and tomorrow draws near, I jot down next to the list of names. I cross out *one way or another* several times but leave the rest of the sentence. *Today passes and tomorrow draws near.*

How will today be remembered?

I took a day off work to etch this day in memory, and tomorrow I'll go and sit behind my desk holding fast to the memory of today. My desk is in the administrative office of a

154   dd's Umbrella

shoe manufacturer specialised in producing inexpensive women's shoes that copy the designs of mid-to-low-range brands. My job consists of managing inventory and paperwork across nationwide retailers. Some of the shoemakers I've befriended are generous enough to make custom-fitted shoes for me now and then, which I appreciate, but I don't know how much longer I'll go on working there. And with that, K pops back into my head like a nasty migraine I can't shake. Somehow he knew I was taking today off, and had made a point of smiling sardonically when he came by to hand me some paperwork. So, Kim Soyoung juim, I hear you're off tomorrow? Why's that then? Going somewhere, are we? You wanted to see for yourself? And what if you do, you think your being there will make a difference? I told K about three months back that I wasn't interested in dating him, and he's taken this tone with me ever since, possibly to wear me down and get me to hand in my notice. It may be that he's trying to tell me he won't be insulted by the likes of me. Yes, that's it, isn't it? He's saying, know how small and feeble and powerless you are.

K's love interest. I don't know how long this label's been stalking me at the office, but by the time I realised that K always found a way to sit beside or across from me, the designation had stuck and people were teasing me about our supposed relationship. I'd deny it, say I was already in a relationship, and then they'd say, Really, well show us then, and I'd say No, why should I show you anything, and they'd say, See, that's what I thought, that proves you're not, you need to forget these imaginary boyfriends who materialise when it's convenient for you and get serious about this man, this living, breathing man right under your nose, and just think, if you hit it off we can all look

Hwang 155

forward to free bowls of noodles at your wedding, won't that be exciting? Through all this K would sit with a self-satisfied grin on his face. Then he made a habit of catching up to me in his car as I left the office. Hop in, I'll drive you home, he'd say out of his car window. Home was six bus stops away and I could easily walk it, so I would decline his offer, but he wouldn't relent, he was there again the next day insisting I get in. I said I preferred to walk, repeatedly, but he'd continue to drive alongside and tell me not to worry, that he wasn't a bad guy.

One day I discovered K waiting for me in the car park even though I'd made sure he left the office ahead of me, and from that day forward I avoided him as best I could and kept myself guarded whenever I spoke to him about work matters, keeping my answers brief and to the point. Sometime after that, on a lunch break, I was having a chat and a coffee with a colleague from the sales team near the entrance to the building when K approached and, addressing the colleague, positioned himself between us. Then, as if to distance me from the colleague, he lightly nudged me aside by briefly wrapping his arm around my waist. Shocked into momentary silence by this physical contact, and because I felt unable to interrupt the discussion that immediately followed about an important deal in the works, I returned to my desk without addressing the incident. After an agonising night, I went to work the next day and summoned K to the stairs. I told him I never wanted to get in his car, never had and never would, and that whatever anyone said, I had no interest in going out with him, ever, so he'd better not touch me again without my consent... Not in these words, I did try to be circumspect, and K, upon hearing this, took a step back and apologised for placing his hand on my back the day before but, he said, he hadn't intended to touch

156   dd's Umbrella

me or anything like that. Then, face burning, he rushed up the stairs. Someone must have been in the staircase above us, because I heard a voice ask, What is it, what's going on? and then I heard K say, Oh, nothing, I think there was some misunderstanding on Kim juim's part.

From that day on I became the target of K's anger and frustration. He stopped addressing me privately, but began to abuse me publicly, barking out orders in an imperious manner and taking his sweet time whenever I requested documents from him. When he found an error in my work he'd march up to my desk and yell in my face, then turn his back to me and stand there fuming, as though rooted to the spot by his rage. It always took a few moments for him to finally walk away. His malicious behaviour didn't go unnoticed, but when the department head tried to dissuade and reason with him, K at first feigned ignorance, then he said, What, are you afraid someone else will quit because of me? From that conversation I gathered that K had an MO, that he'd done this before in this very office. That was the first I'd heard about it. Whereas everyone else, it turned out, had not only known that this had happened before but had pushed K on me, and even now they'll stop by my desk to tell me how drunk or upset or confessional K was over drinks last night. Then they'll ask, but were you not into him, not even a little?

You Yakshas!

When I'm gripped by the urge to scream these words over my monitor at the entire office, I reroute the impulse and buy something for my desk instead, something entirely frivolous and without purpose, something that's useful insofar as it serves no function. My desk is jam-packed with these objects, there's only a small bit of empty space left now. I picture myself quitting the office for good, leaving everything behind as if I'd dropped off the face of the earth overnight. And how my colleagues will be left to deal with everything, all of the knickknacks I deposited on my desk like rabbit droppings each time I was forced to swallow the words in my throat. Who will inherit my palm-sized succulent? It's bound to stick out when they survey my desk, even amid the chaotic microcosm of inane objects. But maybe some of my office mates have secretly been eyeing it.

At first, the cactus resembled a human palm: five short leaves sprouting, like stocky fingers, from the round, broad, bigger leaf. But then the middle stub started outgrowing the rest. Now it's shot up to thirty centimetres, and every day I go to work expecting to see this middle finger destroyed, that someone has finally broken or twisted or sliced it off. I named and labelled the cactus Middle Finger a while back, and for a time it was the centre of attention, people would come by to crack jokes or to marvel or laugh at its bizarre shape. No one so much as mentions it now. I feel an unspoken tension in their silence. They're probably sitting there imagining what it is I must be imagining via my cactus...

No, unni. No one's that interested in other people, and they certainly don't care enough about anyone else to be imagining such things.

This is Kim Sori's take on the matter. She insists that I tell people at work what I'm going through, describe what I'm feeling even if that's likely to mark me as unstable in their eyes, and continue to articulate the sense of psychological and physical threat and anxiety that grips me when K throws a

158   dd's Umbrella

sarcastic comment in my direction, or barks orders at me, or drives his blue Tivoli a little too fast and a little too close past me as I walk home. But I've been there before, I've lived what it is to do exactly that, to speak out.

In December 2002, just before the 16th presidential election, I was working for a manufacturer of home-learning materials. It was my first job. The head of the company suggested we hold a mini event where company employees would take turns speaking on behalf of the candidate they supported out of the three men: Roh Moo-hyun (Millennium Democratic Party), Lee Hoi-chang (Grand National Party), Kwon Young-ghil (Democratic Labour Party). This was in keeping with the overall mood that election season, which I suppose was unusually participatory, partly because of the lingering effects of the World Cup cohosted earlier that year, when so many had experienced the power of the public square and of the crowd. When my turn to speak came and I listed some of the merits of the candidate I supported, a colleague who was then in the sales team, H, booed and jeered at me — then, as if that wasn't insulting enough, made lewd sucking noises as he pushed his left thumb out between his left index and middle fingers and tapped his right thumb around the tip of the left thumb. I had no idea what he was doing or what it meant, I was mostly puzzled and vaguely offended. Only later, after much thought, did it dawn on me: clit-lick.

Did he use that particular gesture to insult me because I'm a woman? I asked.

Seo Sookyung said my gender probably wouldn't have made a difference, and I had to agree. He had intended to insult and humiliate the speaker, to heckle and harass, to insinuate that what I said amounted to clit-lick. But the question remained, why did he think that was offensive?

And where did he pick up the gesture in the first place?

After taking a few days to think about what had occurred, I reported the incident to HR. But instead of asking H to explain his actions, they all looked aghast at me. Cli-what... ? How could you *think* such a thing not to mention speak of it so publicly... ? *I* was what appalled them.

5

Any time I need to remind myself of beauty, I turn to the stars and to books.

Of all the stories I've read about stars, the most beautiful one is Antoine de Saint-Exupéry's account of the time he crash-landed on a plateau. During a period when French air routes were being mapped out across the Sahara, Saint-Exupéry and his postal plane landed on a flat stretch of desert somewhere between Cape Juby and Villa Cisneros, now Dakhla. Saint-Exupéry stumbled on black stones atop that frustum that had once been submerged in water and lain out of human reach for millions of years, and documented the experience by writing a story about it. 'A sheet spread beneath an apple tree can receive only apples; a sheet spread beneath the stars can receive only stardust.' Thus Saint-Exupéry likened the expanse of desert under the skies to a sheet in what now occurs to me is yet another reference to tablecloths. One that's different, but not significantly, from Olav H. Hauge's tablecloth. Apart from the fact that he wrote *The Little Prince* and went missing on a reconnaissance plane during the Second World War, I know nothing about Saint-Exupéry the man or his life, but thanks to this record of his coming upon fragments of meteorites on a desert plateau some three hundred metres

162   dd's Umbrella

above sea-level — 'here is where my adventure became magical, for in a striking foreshortening of time that embraced thousands of years, I had become the witness of this miserly rain from the stars' — I was also able to witness the fiery rain he had seen. And the night sky and stars spanning billions of years. And the high, cold, desolate frustum overlaid by star fragments on this very planet that had carried on rotating, silently, over those same aeons.

In other words, for eternity.

How long a time is a billion years? Considering that the earliest epic poetry we know of is the *Epic of Gilgamesh*, which dates back about four thousand years, and the earliest surviving recorded prose is *The Tale of Genji*, for humans an aeon is as good as eternity. Yet it also holds that an instant of that eternity is witnessed by Saint-Exupéry's tablecloth, by that single sheetlike expanse. So it turns out there's good reason behind my impulse to pick up a book when I want to hold and touch a thing of beauty, to pick up a bound sheaf of paper that somehow always feels warm to the touch. Or to fill my space with books. Virginia Woolf was right in saying women/people need money and a room of one's own to write. People need money and a room of their own. And in that room there must be a space for books.

In this house there are currently about three thousand books. Seo Sookyung and I regularly cull them down to a manageable number. Every January, we put on masks and work gloves and set about dusting and reorganising and selecting books to send out. Books that have been gathering dust on the shelves after their first chapter failed to grab our attention, stories with interesting narrative structures that lack sentences we feel compelled to reread, nonfiction titles written in a tone or style that we found unappealing — we remove these from the shelves and leave them in a pile by the front door for disposal. A few months ago, we went through another bout of sorting and discarding, and more books than ever before disappeared from my shelves.

To decide what to keep and what to throw out, I'll ask myself one question: would I reread it? A simple question but answering it can be a complicated process. Sarah Waters's *Fingersmith* in Choi Yongjoon's translation and Margaret Atwood's *Alias Grace* in Lee Eunseon's translation were both wonderful reads for me, but whereas I was content with a single reading of the first book, two readings still weren't enough for the second. Why is this? Why or rather how is it that a book that makes it through this nebulous, unpredictable ritual one year can be cast aside without regret the following year? Kawabata Yasunari held on for several consecutive years until last year when every one of his books were packed up; John Williams and Kim Seung-wook's *Stoner* barely made the cut last year and wasn't as lucky this time round. What will happen to Sakaguchi Ango next year? Every year there's the added nuisance of books printed on paper so thin the text on the verso and even the next leaf show through, rendering these books illegible regardless of whether I want to read them or not, and of books weighed down with introductions and forewords and blurbs I've no interest in reading. With the latter I have no choice but to tear off the back covers, though this makes them even more unsightly and exasperates me no end, and eventually I'll have to give them up, unless of course I want to hold on to them for a reread, in which case... But enough of that.

164   dd's Umbrella

At the end of the day books are a necessity for me and having more of them is a good thing, although having a few less is fine by me too, or perhaps the fewer there are the better, and it's with this thought that I sort and select and keep them from spilling out of my room. When I want to buy a book, I wait until I've finished reading at least a couple from the existing stack. The problem, however, is that books go out of print much too quickly, so my reading is always fuelled by a certain amount of urgency towards the next book. What if the book I have my sights on vanishes before I finish reading this one? This isn't purely hypothetical as this actually did happen with the translation of Stanisław Lem's *Solaris*, so reading, for me, is never an entirely carefree, leisurely pursuit.

Will I ever get around to finishing a story of my own, a story to shelve next to the others?

The living room of the house where Kim Sori and I spent our childhood adolescence was cool and had dark brown wood floors. A bookcase with glass doors stood against the north wall, lined with books we had received as hand-me-downs from our cousins. Of these, the most special were the ones in the Boys' and Girls' World Literature Series published by Kyemongsa: the 1976 edition, which comprised fifty volumes, mostly in mint condition and carrying illustrations that were beautifully rough. Each volume was encased in a red strawboard shell and the covers were also of stiff strawboard, while the pages inside were of poor quality and smelled of barley meal and corn bread. It was from rereading those volumes that I developed my lifelong attachment to the materiality of books. I would carefully observe the burrs left where type had pressed upon paper, and as I had a habit of

Hwang   165

rubbing each page as I read, the books I was especially fond of had rounded top corners that made them look old and weathered.

I went through the series and based on the first few pages of each volume and the quality of the printing on those pages, separated the interesting ones from the uninteresting ones and handed the latter off to Kim Sori. Thus *Greek Mythology*, *Homer's Tales*, and *The Bible Story* went to Kim Sori, while *The Strange Travels of Nils*, *The Prince of Stars*, *Scandinavian Fairy Tales*, and *French Fairy Tales* remained with me. Kim Sori didn't so much as lay a finger on the books I'd designated as hers, nor did she touch any of the books I claimed as my own. To this day she brings up those books as proof of how greedy and selfish I can be, and of the impact this had, that *I* had, on her emotional development. And I'll counter by saying that was a long time ago, that I've come a long way since, and besides, didn't I effectively shield her childhood from Hans Christian Andersen? From the grim world of that hateful writer who had a destitute girl be ostracised by grown-ups and abandoned by god, then had her feet chopped off, then had her live enslaved to terror in a rectory, and then, and only then, finally granted her entry into heaven? All because she happened to covet a pair of pretty red shoes.

There's a rumour that Andersen was bisexual and if that's true, I find it puzzling how someone who must have led a life restricted by social taboos could have written such a terrible and punishing tale about the breaking of taboos. How did he wind up the father of fairy tales on the basis of such a story? In any case, I have zero patience for stories where mothers speak motherhood and fathers speak taboo. I've no patience for adults who, drunk on such stories, read them to children. I want Jung

166   dd's Umbrella

Jinwon to grow up reading better stories. Since the experience
of reading is also the experience of receiving in our palms the
words of the lives that came before us, i.e., the forms of life of
previous generations. I came across a line to that effect recently,
in a book by Roland Barthes, I think. Yes, it was Barthes. 'To
live [...] is to receive the *forms* of the life of the sentences that
preexist us'.

Our family fell into hard times just as Kim Sori was finishing
middle school and I was in high school. We realised how
fucked we were, how impoverished we'd become when all the
books Kim Sori and I owned, including the Boys' and Girls'
World Literature Series, were taken from us. Strange men
barged in one day and stomped around in their shoes shutting
the doors of our cabinets and shelves, including the bookcase,
then sealed the doors with seizure stickers. If we attempted to
take anything out, the torn stickers would prove our
noncompliance.

Ma wasn't home, she'd been gone since early morning, and
Pa had just left for work as well, so Kim Sori and I were alone
at home. After the bailiffs had stamped through the house
leaving a trail of shoe prints and stickers, the phone rang. Have
they left? It was Pa. As he walked out he'd passed a group of
men headed in the direction of our home and intuited that
they were bailiffs. I realised that Pa had been outside the whole
time, that he'd left us children alone to deal with the situation.
I was furious and shouted at him, but he told me he'd made a
quick determination that it was better if he were absent given
the situation, that on that assessment he'd waited for them to
finish their job and leave. He said his 'power' would have made
matters worse and caused an even greater tragedy. At the time

Kim Sori and I believed his assessment to have been an actual assessment, but we no longer consider this to be true. Would having him or an adult man at home in such a situation only have led to more trouble? Truly? Isn't that merely inflated self-belief or exaggerated self-doubt?

Our pa's one of those people who claims to have first-hand experience of everything. Born in 1946 as the eldest son of five daughters and two sons, he started various small businesses before he was twenty, but as he had no nose for trade every venture ended in failure, leaving him to borrow off his older and younger sisters who all earned money working as *mising sida*, slaving under sewing machinists. Grandma, who had lost her husband in the war and thereafter raised her children with what she earned at the market, did not blame her son for these failures; for her these were not proofs of incompetence, but evidence of his misfortune and innate character. And this was how his sisters viewed him as well for the longest time. The businesses not panning out were just the consequence of him being the good-hearted younger brother he was, who didn't have the capacity to deceive or harm; or being the poor older brother whose losing streak wouldn't abate and who was constantly brought to his knees by the cold, merciless world of business; or being the good poor son down on his luck. Pa was more than used to seeing himself in this light, not to mention expert at presenting himself as such. When the subject comes up, he speaks of the bailiff incident of 1992 — which had a tremendous psychological impact on my sister and me — as his own, framing it as *his* experience. He'll say: Do you know what it was like for me in 1992 when the bailiffs turned up at our door? You can't imagine what hell I went through, how tortuous it was to stand in the phone box outside smoking

168 dd's Umbrella

cigarette after cigarette. Yes, of course, Pa. You're right, it must
have been really tough for you. Kim Sori and I were often
overcome by pity for him, all throughout our adolescence and
early adulthood, and even up to a few years ago. I think back
on this now and wonder what became of that pity. Where did
it go? What happened to us, to our hearts? I've no doubt Pa
wonders this, too. What's gotten into my daughters? When did
they become so critical? And so *sensitive*?

Pa sells portable heaters and air-conditioners in his shop on the
first floor of Sewoon Market in Jangsadong, Jongno. Heaters
and coolers don't bring in enough money, so he's got an array
of home appliances as well: humidifiers, toasters, electric kettles
and the like. Actual sales don't compare to what they were
thirty or forty years ago, but he seems to get by, earning just
enough to cover the rent on the shop and the living costs of
two people. The overall landscape around his shop and the
electronics market area hasn't changed a whole lot. The brands
and the designs on display may be different, but what I see
from his shop is more or less the landscape I saw ten, twenty,
thirty years ago. Pa started the shop in Sewoon Market with
money from his eldest sister, the eldest daughter of the Kims,
who got a visa and fled to America saying she'd had her fill of
life in Korea, but not before handing him the money she'd
saved up one last time. And though he did go bankrupt at one
point, Pa has managed over the last four decades to more or
less carry on and in the same location too. His shop faces the
car park, which is always dark because the second-floor deck
blocks out natural light, and is full of the stench of cigarettes,
car exhaust, spit, and piss.

This was where Pa was back in 1987, when he used to commute to work on the bus that passed through Gwanghwamun and deposited him at Jongno-3-ga. One night in June of that year, Ma went to meet Pa on his way home, something she rarely did. Later that night, they came back reeking of chilli powder. They stumbled inside as soon as the door opened, and Kim Sori and I recoiled at the acrid air that tumbled in with them, a smell that was familiar yet entirely new to us. It filled the house the moment they stepped in the door, and Kim Sori and I had difficulty breathing. Seeing our parents' watery eyes and runny noses, their cheeks swollen and red from scratching, we were afraid, we thought something terrible must have happened to them on the way home as it appeared they'd both been weeping, but no, they couldn't be more cheerful. They kept saying *those people, those people* before dissolving into fits of laughter, peals erupting out of them each time their eyes met and again as they caught a glimpse of our confused gaping faces, and then they'd snort just because, because their faces stung and because their calves were sore from all the running. We had never seen our parents share such an intimate moment of hilarious joy, nor would we ever again. Eventually they peeled off their rank clothes, chucked them in the washing machine, and headed to the bathroom to wash, giggling like children. The sharp scent had seeped into their hair and was impossible to wash out with a shower, and as this scene repeated itself over the course of the next few days, the smell got into their pillows and blankets and lingered for days afterwards in their bedroom and the bedding cabinet. That was our first encounter with tear gas.

170   dd's Umbrella

Back in 1996, when I returned home after the Yonsei incident, Pa greeted me warmly and began to describe his own experience — his *history* as he put it — of hurling rocks at state power, which naturally segued into what he witnessed in Jongno and Gwanghwamun in June of 1987. He was on his way home when he caught sight of police spraying tear gas at a crowd of people shouting Revise the Constitution, Overthrow the Dictatorship, and this so enraged him that he started shouting at the police, Hey, you, police, stop that, stop with the beating, stop with the tear gas — and the next thing he knew, he was smack in the middle of Jongno-3-ga throwing rocks and marching with the others, in the very rank and file of the democracy movement which was not only instrumental in securing direct presidential elections and a constitutional court, but also in prompting the constitutional revisions that reduced the president's authority (including revoking the authority to dissolve the National Assembly) while increasing that of the National Assembly (by granting it the authority to lift martial law and to audit the government). Yes, he had been there too — but nowadays, well, the times were different now. Times these days, *your* time. He sat cross-legged on the floor in shorts and an undershirt, a pack of This and a cheap lighter on the floor in front of him. It was his habit to light a cigarette the moment he sat down, but that day he didn't once reach for his cigarettes or the lighter for as long as he spoke. What have you got to protest about, he said in an agonised voice. You don't live under a dictatorship. You live in an era when even Chun Doo-hwan has been locked up. You have no cause. Stop raising those flags. Stop following the protestors. Agitators. Look how they're all scrambling to go to North Korea. This is all their doing, the Reds.

That my parents played a part in the June 1987 Democracy Movement was a tale I'd been told for as long as I could remember: We were there in Gwanghwamun, your ma and pa, neither of us had seen such a large group of people before — and the police suddenly started firing tear gas directly into the packed crowd, *pa-pap pa-pap-pap-pap*, and instantly, within seconds, panic and mayhem, everyone scattering, shrieking, sobbing.

It pains me to think of what immediately followed, that what my parents witnessed on the back of June 1987 was the rift between leading opposition figures Kim Dae-jung (27 per cent of votes) and Kim Young-sam (28 per cent of votes), and the subsequent election of Chun's successor Roh Tae-woo (with 36.6 per cent of the votes on 16 December, 1987, in the country's 13th presidential election). In 1987 they would both have been forty-one, as I am now, which makes it all the more poignant. What went through their minds that December? How did they feel about the election? Did they consider the movement a failure? Would they have felt that protesting had achieved nothing, that it had been a fool's errand, its outcomes predictable? Did the experience mark them thereafter?

*

Hannah Arendt, in writing about the 1961 trial of Eichmann in Jerusalem, elaborates on the 'three closely interrelated inabilities of Eichmann [...] the inability to speak, or to think, or to stand in someone else's shoes.' (Kim Sunwook, 'Translator's Preface' in Hannah Arendt, *Eichmann in Jerusalem,* Hangilsa, 2006). The word 'banality' is translated as 평범성, ordinariness, in the Korean edition, but as Hak-Ie Kim has pointed out, seems

172   dd's Umbrella

closer in meaning to 상투성, triteness. ('Though the majority of Korean scholars translate "banality" as "ordinariness", this does not seem quite fitting. [...] Arendt interpreted this idea as "thoughtlessness" in the afterword to the 1965 revised edition. Here "thoughtlessness" refers to a state of thinness where true communication is impossible due to the use of conventional turns of phrase. And is therefore trite and predictable', Hak-Ie Kim, 'Translator's Foreword' in Raul Hilberg, *The Destruction of the European Jews*, Kaemagowon, 2008.) The aspect of evil Arendt observed in Eichmann likely had its origin in the cliché rather than in the ordinary.

Followers of North Korea and Leftist Reds.

In Pa's words, which echo the tone and stance and lexicon of the newspaper he's subscribed to for decades, I hear the Eichmann-like platitudes Arendt described. The inability, that is, to speak, or to think, or to empathise.

Pa is now in his seventies and is lost unless his table is set for him, forgets which drawers hold his socks and which his trousers, neglects to wash or to take care of himself when he's ill and drives Ma into a frenzied anxiety, blames his daughters for abandoning him, and generally spends a considerable amount of time resenting and reviling someone or something. He is resentful of both youth and old age, but most of all he detests unions and whistleblowers and Roh Moo-hyun — because strikes are commie activities, because the lawyer Kim Yong-chul who disclosed Samsung's alleged slush fund worth billions of won is an underhanded traitor, and because the late Roh Moo-hyun was a mediocre man who managed to clamber up to an absurd level of power. What do they need unions and strikes for, he complains, when they earn a lot more than I do for manual labour, and in his complaint there is simultaneously an antipathy towards labour and labourers and a deep-seated aversion of weakness, and considering that one of his oft-repeated assertions as regards former president Roh Moo-hyun is *He has no authority, nothing*, it would seem that his contempt for labourers, for Kim Yong-chul, and for Roh Moo-hyun stems from one source — or so we figure. What he hates is the lack of authority. His contempt is a contempt of powerlessness. He detests weakness.

But what is power and what is authority according to him? This question never fails to remind me of the tin-plated floor table our family had back in the 1980s, a circular dinner table with fold-out legs, its silvery face imprinted with a colourful array of flowers, leaves, and peacocks. On the day Seo Seon-ang won the gold medal in gymnastics at the 1986 Asian Games, we were eating dinner around that same table. (Gold medallist Seo Seon-ang retired not long after the 1986 Asian Games due to an injury that prevented her from entering the 1988 Seoul Olympics.) Seo Seon-ang's balance beam event was shown on the news, and towards the end of the broadcast we saw images of Chun Doo-hwan and Lho Shin-yong. (Lho Shin-yong was the 18th prime minister of Korea who stepped down in 1987 after the death of student activist Park Jong-chul sparked the June Democracy Movement.) Hoping to impress him, I said, Pa, if the president dies the prime minister becomes the president, right? — at which my pa hurriedly reached across the table and clamped his hand over my mouth. I'd only wanted to show off what I knew, but he told me I shouldn't speak of such things, that if I went around saying such things soldiers would come and take him away. He was visibly terrified.

Let's assume, then, that the authority Pa speaks of is synonymous with power, and that this power is capable of

174   dd's Umbrella

striking people with terror. A power that leads a man to silence his child in the privacy of their home: this was the sort of power he had intimate experience of, understood, and came to equate with all power. He cannot stand the absence of such power. He cannot stand a 'lack of authority'. He fears his own lack of authority for this lack cannot inflict fear on anyone. When he attacks another for this perceived lack, he derives a certain 'authority' — the authority to condemn — and so he musters all his strength into hatred, towards any and all forms of powerlessness.

Pa seems to have determined that the quarrel with his daughters stems from our different political views, and if that is an actual determination, I can agree. Kim Sori and I trace the tangible germ of this ongoing tension back to the day my parents first met their soon-to-be in-laws, in the lead-up to Kim Sori's wedding. Kim Sori married a fabric distributor of the family name Jung five years ago. Pa wasn't thrilled with the choice and made his disapproval known, and Ma and Kim Sori and I worried that he would be spiteful enough to behave as usual on the day itself, but he was the picture of gracious decorum, an attitude we'd never seen in him before. The difficult part over, we were driving back home when Pa started to vent his indignation at Mr. Jung's earlier suggestion that the two of them go for drinks, that he would drop by Jongno soon. And why would I agree to see him if he did? Pa said loudly, Does he think I've nothing better to do than be at his beck and call? How presumptuous, how *smug*! Does he think since he's got a son, he's got it all? The gloating look on his face! Smiling like he's won.

How can I explain the chill that went through us in that

moment? Kim Sori and I were sitting up front, she behind the wheel and I in the passenger seat, and when we heard his words we froze. In that moment, Pa had revealed a sense of inferiority he'd evidently been nursing all these decades, letting slip his true opinion on having sons — though one could argue that seeing as both of his daughters were fully grown and had reached adulthood without an inkling of his real feelings, this lapse was on the contrary a testament to what a relatively decent father he had been. At least that's what Seo Sookyung and Kim Sori and I would say later as we discussed the events of the day. But it is also true that since that day, since he revealed his hand with the words *smiling like he's won,* Kim Sori and I have been unable to consider our relationship to our pa in the same light. Once we knew, there was no going back. How could we? When we'd realised that our very existence was part and parcel of the supposed misfortune that plagued poor Pa. Or to be more precise, the fact of our vaginas.

What Pa considers most unjust in his daughters' behaviour towards him may be the fact that they no longer appear to pity him. He knows how closely we follow social issues and how much we care about social justice, and he makes a point of demonstrating his disapproval and condemning our ingratitude and treachery in putting strangers before kin. He saw our concern for the survivors of Sewol ferry, which sank off Paengmok Port on the island of Jindo on 16 April, 2014. He saw how closely we followed news of the families of the dead and the as yet unfound, and took all this to heart. He assumed we were motivated by pity. He would say, How can you care that much about people you've never met when you won't look after your own parents? Isn't that morally wrong, a

176   dd's Umbrella

contradiction? First tend to your own front yard, I always say.

I wonder if we should tell him we've cottoned on to the fact that by *front yard* he means no one else's front yard but his own. Pa lets us know through regular messages relayed through Ma that he is furious now, furious with his daughters for being so serious about his harmless jokes, for not agreeing with him when he says, Don't you pity your poor Pa, for no longer caring, for being angry all the time. If you insist on treating me like this I won't forgive either one of you, he supposedly said, but what good is his forgiveness? His forgiveness... We simply have no use for it. It pains me that he fails to realise this or refuses to accept it. The truth is that whenever we sit down to think about our parents as I'm doing now, Kim Sori and I realise we are not so much angry as heartbroken.

Ma continues to call us, trying to patch things up and end the stalemate. Your father is so cross and irritable these days, he won't leave me alone, when I go out I make sure there's a soup prepared, I tell him all he has to do is get the banchan out from the fridge when he's hungry, but when I get back I find he's eaten only the rice and kimchi and left everything else out on the table with the lids off as if to criticise my cooking, as if he's saying, Look at what I had to eat. That's what I have to deal with and it's really too much, I can't take it anymore, she sighs, then pleads: Couldn't the two of you calm him down, be sweet to your pa, would you, please? Before ending, as always, on the same note: Won't you take pity on your poor ma?

In *Imaginary Athens: Urban Space and Memory in Berlin, Tokyo, and Seoul,* Jin-Sung Chun explains the concept of 'kokutai' or national polity as referenced by the Constitution of the Empire of Japan, which came into effect in 1890. In arguing that the emperor is the 'hollow core' of Japanese national polity, he draws on Kitaro Nishida's concept of 'absolute nothingness' and describes a 'logic [that] predicates a religious state in which subject and object become one without being hindered any more by reason' and which 'leaves open the possibility to regard the Japanese people as a subject that is dissolved into an object called empire. In [which] case, the absolute nothingness that transcends subject and object, would, of course, be the emperor.' Reading this I was reminded of *The End of Evange lion*, the 1997 animated film based on the *Neon Genesis Evangelion* TV series. Ikari Gendo, father of Ikari Shinji and the head of the paramilitary organisation and manufacturer of fighter cyborgs known as NERV, and who in the TV series had remained inscrutably stolid and silent throughout, reveals his true desire in the film adaptation. He risks the Third Impact to reunite with his wife Ikari Yui, who has been absorbed into Evangelion Unit 01, and all of humanity including Gendo pays the price for his pure unimpeachable love by being turned into a single liquid consciousness. In a world now emptied of humans, EVA Unit 01 pilot Ikari Sihnji and Unit 02 pilot Soryu Asuka Langley survive as the last of humankind. The film ends with Asuka's words. In a world tinged in orange and suffering the consequences of his father's actions, Shinji weeps, and Asuka says: *Kimochi warui. I feel sick.*

6

How will Jung Jinwon remember us? Kim Sori, Seo Sookyung, me: the adults gathered here today.

Adults. When did we become adults?

When Jung Jinwon was born, I paid several visits to the hospital and to the postnatal care facility. Not because I found my first nibling particularly beautiful, but because their tiny, weeks-old face resembled no one else's I knew. How could a face unlike any other face feel this familiar? Intrigued and awed and somewhat frightened by this, I visited as often as I could. Usually the baby would be lying in a clear plastic cot, wrapped up in swaddling clothes like a pupa. Asleep or awake, cranky or puckering their chapped lips. I thought back to when this face hadn't yet arrived in my life, to when I had neither expected nor predicted its existence, all the way back to when Kim Sori and I were children ourselves, as well as all the times between then and now... Searching my memory, thinking I must have come across this face before. The very next day, I'd feel an urge to go back and stare some more. Day by day, the infantile face grew into itself, as a butterfly's wings unfurl when it emerges from its cocoon, and I wondered if one day I would glimpse something in their face that would remind me of where I'd come across its likeness before.

180   dd's Umbrella

Jung Jinwon is five years old now and speaks in subject-verb sentences. But when they first began to speak, they built their vocabulary around a single word: *pretty*. Fish pretty, they would say. Butterfly pretty. Mama pretty. Mama pretty today. Nini eyes pretty today. On weekends or weekday evenings, I am sometimes left in charge of the child, meaning I am left alone with them, and I'm often at a loss. I have no idea what we could possibly do together. Playing is hard and conversation especially hard. How is anyone supposed to talk to a child and how does one answer their questions? I am bewildered, distressed. I fear the impact my words will have. One day the two of us happened to walk past a dried-up potted plant left out in the street. I couldn't tell if the intent was to revive or kill it, but as we passed by Jung Jinwon asked if the tree was dead. It's alive, for now, I said. Then, realising my answer leaned closer to death than to life, I glanced down with a mixture of guilt and panic. But Jinwon looked fine, even if they were squinting at the bright sunlight. Their face was earnest, as though they were weighing something in their mind. I hoped our exchange wouldn't leave a lasting impression, that it was forgotten within moments.

A similar thing happened the year before last when we were reading Jon Klassen's *This Is Not My Hat*, translated by Seo Nam-hee. In the book, a fish steals a hat then tries to find a place to hide it. The fish swims along, unaware that a bigger fish, the hat's owner, is trailing behind, before slipping inside some seaweed, convinced it has found the perfect hiding spot. The big fish follows behind. The next page shows the big fish make its way serenely out of the thicket of seaweed having reclaimed its hat. The final page shows only the seaweed. When we got to this page Jung Jinwon became visibly upset.

They pulled the book closer and leafed through the pages again from front to back and back to front, then they attempted to tear the book open, as if there might be a page tucked between the last page and the back cover, or inside the glued inner side of the back cover. They were trying to find the hidden story. Eventually, they asked me where the fish had gone. I couldn't answer. I had found the ending surprising too. The forest of seaweed on the last page looked so peaceful, and I understood it as an allusion to the narrator's death. The death of the little fish. We could only see black, brown, and reddish plants on the last page, but I thought the author and illustrator might have hidden the little fish's body somewhere among the plants. It had to be in there somewhere. I looked a second and a third time, convinced I could find it. Jung Jinwon kept crying and asking where the fish had gone, and I felt flustered and entirely useless, I could only say that the little fish was either dead or must have been gobbled up by the big fish.

When Jung Jinwon and I grumbled about the book later, Seo Sookyung laughed.

But the little fish is only hiding.

Why is it hiding?

Because it's ashamed. It will come out soon enough.

When though?

When you're not looking, when no one's looking.

*

Shame is what turns one into an adult, Kim Sori had said a few months ago.

182   dd's Umbrella

She had dropped by my office for lunch. We started reminiscing about our childhood, and when I mentioned the smell of tear gas filling our doorway back in June 1987, Kim Sori cocked her head and said she didn't remember that. For her, tear gas was linked to the summer of 1996. That summer Kim Sori was a student at a commercial high school and had a part-time job at a fast-food place near Hongik University. One day after work, she boarded a bus near Hapjeong Station, and a group of university students shouted and gestured frantically at her to get off the bus. She didn't understand what was going on. The students had bands and torn clothes scribbled with writing tied around their heads and chests, their faces were smudged with dirt and sweat, and some had ripped the arms off their shirts. In short, all of them looked so out of place that Kim Sori thought they must be in costume; then she remembered the demonstrations happening in Shinchon. She realised they were trying to get her to take another bus since they reeked of tear gas. But she had to get home. She had to take that bus, and she'd already paid the fare. Kim Sori was flustered, then annoyed. By the students' concerned faces, by their kindness that verged on condescension, and by how these older unnis and oppas seemed to be suggesting she stay away because the words written on their bands and on their bodies, words like *Minjok* and *Democracy* had nothing at all to do with *her*. Who are you to tell me what I can or cannot do, which bus I can or cannot take? Feeling both proud and resentful, Kim Sori found an empty seat, sat down, and started crying as the bus crossed Yanghwa Bridge. The entire car was permeated with the chemicals coating the hair and clothing of the older students. It stank so bad, Kim Sori recalled.

I regretted getting on the bus, but I couldn't let them see that of course so I stayed put in my seat and wept. They were pretending to be adults, I thought. When they were, what, three or four years older than me at most? And were only in uni because they'd been given that opportunity, and now they're acting like they're all grown, like they're the adults? To me? That pissed me off. Fuck this, I thought. I didn't know you were there that day too. When I saw you come home looking like a ghost, I teared up again. But the following year, you quit uni. You could even quit uni if you wanted. You didn't even seem that torn up about it. That pissed me off too.

People in uni didn't count as adults in Kim Sori's eyes. Neither did her sibling, her ma, her pa. She only knew one person in her teens who was a proper grown-up, she said, and that was Jihye unni. Bae Jihye had gotten a job straight out of high school, at a warehouse discount store. Bae Jihye was not one to mince words, she spoke her mind regardless of the other person's gender or status, and she was quick to size up a situation and deal with it. Kim Sori learned the ropes of the new job from Bae Jihye, and received both praise and encouragement for the work she did. She shadowed Bae Jihye to learn the ins and outs of the job, or more precisely the way she approached the work, and this earned her nicknames like Jihye's Spawn or Baby Jihye, but she didn't mind. She liked these names because it felt good to be associated with Bae Jihye and because it suggested that she was becoming more like Jihye: good at her job, responsible, dependable, consistent, a grown-up who wouldn't be looked down on or ignored, at least not in her own field.

184   dd's Umbrella

Kim Sori told me an anecdote about how Bae Jihye once caught an eleven-year-old kid stealing. The kid had been roaming around the store alone. She brought the child to the Information Desk and asked, Why were you stealing? The child said, Ma's at home, she's sick, but it's something she really needs so I had to steal it for her. When Bae Jihye pointed out that the stolen item was a part for a plastic model kit and surely of no use to a sick ma, the child said, But I'm telling the truth, Ma said she really, really needed it and I wanted to bring it to her. Bae Jihye looked at the child in disbelief, then said, Right, fine, piss off then, and walked off. Kim Sori saw the whole scene, saw the child stand there, dazed, before looking about as if to make sure they really were off the hook, then slink off somewhere. Kim Sori was nineteen at the time.

Kim Sori worked there for another three years, during which she and her coworkers went from being directly employed to being employed through a subcontractor, had their contracts extended twice, and then, once that period was up, had to go in search of another job. Kim Sori lost touch with Bae Jihye after that, but she had picked up some elements of the 'Bae Jihye method', as she called it, at work, and claimed that anyone who followed this method became highly competent. What would Jihye unni do? This was the question Kim Sori asked herself in all that she did as a productive member of society. And so in 2009, when she saw two eleven-year-old kids using a box cutter to rip open the clear wrapping on a comic book in the bookshop in Mokdong, Yangcheongu, where she was working, Kim Sori said she didn't even have to ask the question, she knew what Jihye unni would do.

The kids had been careless with the box cutter and shredded through the cover, Kim Sori said. Another five copies, also ripped through, lay about their feet. The box cutter had the shop's price tag on it, they'd clearly picked it up at the stationary corner. How could you? I asked, and they said they wanted to know what happens next in the story but had no money. They cried and pleaded with me not to call their ma. I was angry but somewhat bewildered, and then I felt a coolness settle right behind my eyes. I said to them: Right, fine.

Piss off then.

And I went back to the till. The kids stood about awkwardly. Eventually they stopped crying and left the store. I talked to a colleague working the cash register about the damaged books. We couldn't return them, the publisher wouldn't take back ruined copies. That's when a man approached the register. I knew him slightly. From the customer information we had on file, I knew he was born in 1962 and a registered member of the bookshop, and I remembered that he'd said he was a maths teacher when he put in an order with me for some magazines that summer. He told me he'd seen what happened and that it had shamed him deeply, that he hoped I knew how disgracefully I'd acted to those children as the adult.

I don't remember his face, strangely enough. All I have is a vague impression of a doughy face, dark round eyes, round nose, mouth. Maybe he looked me up and down as he spoke, maybe he laughed. I couldn't speak and stood gaping in silence. Thankfully my colleague stepped in to defend me and to explain how frequently kids pocket or deface books. We have to call them out when we can and shame them a little, because otherwise the situation can get out of hand, my colleague

186   *dd's Umbrella*

added. This only made me more ashamed. I wished the man would leave, please just turn and walk away. And I wished my colleague would stop talking, stop explaining! I was twenty-nine. I've never talked about this to anyone since, unni. My colleague and I never discussed it again and I wanted to forget the whole thing. But it would pop back into my head at random moments. Late at night, or in quiet moments.

Why did I react like that?

Why did *I* have to feel ashamed?

As the adult. Meaning what?

How does one become an adult anyway? Simply by growing up and reaching a certain age?

Am I an adult?

Has anyone ever let me be one?

These questions looped endlessly in my head and everything felt so unfair. I wanted to forget the whole thing, but I had no one to talk to about any of it and couldn't let it go for the longest time... The thing is, Jihye unni was twenty-one back then. Only two years older than me. Which isn't to say she didn't deserve all the respect I had for her, because the Jihye unni I met straight out of school was definitely an adult. What was *I*, though, at twenty-nine? At thirty-four? This is what unsettled me. That at twenty-nine I'd copied the actions of a twenty-one-year-old — someone I'd found mature and had looked up to as an adult, sure, but *at nineteen*. And that's when I finally saw those two kids. All that time I'd focused only on the man and myself, and I saw then that it wasn't about me or my humiliation, but about how I treated those children. If someone ever asks me about the most shameful moment of my life, that day would top the list. I'm not even ashamed, not really, about relying on you financially, unni — but I am

Hwang 187

mortified about telling a couple of kids to piss off. And that's why, that's how I know now that I'm an adult.

*

After lunch, I said goodbye to Kim Sori and returned to my office in a rage. I was furious at the man. The maths teacher born in 1962 who used to frequent a bookshop in Mokdong, Yangcheongu, in the early 2000s. I knew I could never forgive him. In my anger, I could barely make out the draft order on my desk, which I had to send down to the factories that afternoon.

Why did I react like that?

For years, Kim Sori had tormented herself with this question, but what about him? Did *he* torment himself? Did *he* feel plagued by questions he couldn't answer? Or was he at peace, certain that he'd acted in fairness and with every right? He'd said Kim Sori should realise the disgracefulness of her actions, but what Kim Sori had been made to feel, what she took away from that encounter was humiliation and contempt. He demanded maturity from her despite being the elder, yet he hadn't shared any part of the adult responsibility he demanded of her, no, he'd only finger-wagged and walked away. *His* adulthood only kicked in as he observed and determined Kim Sori to be lacking in maturity, and as he approached — after the fact — to berate her. But if that's what being a grown-up is, isn't it a little too convenient and a little too vile? All afternoon and evening these thoughts followed me around, and after failing to fall asleep that night, I walked over to Seo Sookyung's room to tell her how petty and despicable I thought the man was, how I couldn't stand the thought of him.

188   dd's Umbrella

Yeah, you're right, it was petty of him, Seo Sookyung said. She empathised with Kim Sori's humiliation and my fury, then she said: If Kim Sori came to realise what it means to be an adult as her humiliation turned to shame, and given that Sori herself seems to value that experience, don't you think the maths teacher was an important part of that process too? After all, it was his words that prompted what followed. And as he happened to be at the store by chance, do you think maybe he was doing what he could in the situation? Maybe that was *his* best?

I went back to bed weighed down with these additional questions. Sleep was impossible. The teacher may have served as an 'incentive', but of a tragic sort, I thought. If he was instrumental to Kim Sori's wising up, was Kim Sori instrumental in the two kids growing up to become responsible adults? They were dealt the same humiliation as her. Shame, scorn, and mortification can and do shape a person into an adult, but if these feelings also make you wish the witnesses to your actions would *just leave*, what sort of adult does that make you? What sort of person are you if your maturation is prompted by ugly feelings and random run-ins? These thoughts kept me awake — no, if I'm honest, what kept me up was the fact that my anger, the reason I couldn't find it in myself to forgive that teacher, was related to my distress at the fact that my sister's own adulthood had been shaped by such a troubling experience.

7

'[T]o live is to speak. [...] to live [...] is to receive the *forms* of the life of the sentences that preexist us'. Since coming across these words in Roland Barthes's *The Preparation of the Novel*, I've been trying to savour each and every sentence in the book. I microdose on them; I've been poring over the same book for over a year. Having meditated on Japanese culture in *Empire of Signs*, Barthes once again reveals a penchant for Japanese culture in his analysis of haiku in *The Preparation of the Novel*. In *Imaginary Athens: Urban Space and Memory in Berlin, Tokyo, and Seoul*, Jin-Sung Chun determines Barthes's analysis of Japanese culture to be an 'excessively creative misinterpretation', but, to me, Barthes's analysis seems less an analysis of Japan or what Barthes himself called 'an enormous labour of knowledge [about the Orient]', but rather, and foremost, an analysis of his own tastes/aesthetics, and it was this aspect that kindled my affinity to his work. A sort of mania or experience of awe not unlike my own experience of awe towards the page and the book... I glimpsed the euphoric countenance of an obsessive *otaku* in his sentences.

The front cover of *The Last Lecture*, the Korean edition of *The Preparation of the Novel* translated by Byon Gwang-bae, features Barthes's face. In the photograph Barthes is smoking a cigar, and when you peel off the black-and-white dust jacket,

190   dd's Umbrella

the inner hardcover, surprisingly enough, is of a light purple colour. I removed the outer cover as soon as I bought the book, and light purple, not black and white, is the colour I've come to associate with the volume. It is, of all the books I own, the *most* unambiguously light purple. What would Barthes make of the fact that his last 'words' were bound in a light *murasaki* colour? I tend to think he would have read Murasaki Shikibu's *The Tale of Genji*, and that he would have known the word *murasaki* meant purple or lavender. When I first saw the light purple hardcover, I turned the book over in my hand and wondered how much of an influence his being gay might have had on the publisher's decision to choose that particular colour for the cover of his lecture notes, but now I wonder why I wondered such a thing.

When I mentioned this to Seo Sookyung, she said she'd had the same thought, that though purple is not generally seen as a queer colour here, there is sufficient association to queerness that she also felt it may have been a factor in their decision. We tried to trace the origin of this felt truth, and wound up discussing Boradori from the *Teletubbies*, which was first broadcast in 1998 on the public TV station KBS. The show was a global sleeper hit, winning over fans of all ages, and though the serene and strange daily activities that unfolded on the hills of Teletubbyland lacked logic and causality, once you saw the program you were bound to keep watching — and this addictive quality had led to several conspiracy theories being put forward, including the theory that Boradori was gay. Boradori's droopy swaying movements (which, to be fair, was how all Teletubbies move) and the fact that purple was a mix of blue and red, were said to prove this claim. The intent was to expose the viewing public to gayness through this friendly and familiar character on a children's show, and brainwash us into thinking the gays were lovely and harmless. Had Seo Sookyung and I been affected by these pseudo theories without realising?

In any case, this lavender book is paired in my study with a pink book, a book that happens to be the largest tome I own: *The Better Angels of Our Nature*, which, at this moment, is on the table alongside Barthes's book.

I take pleasure in thinking the colour of the Korean edition's cover of *The Better Angels of Our Nature* is a nod to the author's name. The English editions of this book, both the hardcover published in 2011 and the later paperback, sport no pink at all; the paperback's cover features a rusted, dirty razor blade that looks intractable and hazardous. There are no baby angels either, in contrast to the Korean edition cover which features eight of them. Are baby angels 'better angels'? In the book, Steven Pinker addresses the brutality pervasive in Christian cultures founded on the Hebrew Bible. How to explain the baby angels on the cover of the Korean edition then? There was a brief period in my life when I was compelled by my parents to attend a Protestant church and some fragmented impressions have left their mark, including a vague residual fear of idol worship, which may explain why when I first came across this cover, I did not find the association of goodness with angels or infants to be incongruous or disconcerting. By what processes do people associate one thing with another? How do unconscious or unthinking associations arise, and what part does what's generally referred to as common sense play in that process? How do ideas like *good* and *angel* and *baby*, against a pink backdrop, interact and relate?

192   dd's Umbrella

Whatever anyone says, the history of humanity has progressed away from violence and towards good, to the extent 'we may be living in the most peaceable era in our species' existence.' That Steven Pinker tried very hard to come up with the evidence to support this assertion fills me with a sense of wonder and awe, but the pinkness of his book also always reminds me of the pink triangle, Rosa Winkel. (Could the reverse triangle shape of Boradori's antenna have any connection to the pink triangle?)

Near the Holocaust Memorial in Berlin, across Ebertstrasse, there is a park on the edge of which stands a block of concrete, slightly askew as though it had been hurled into air before landing there. This is the Memorial to Homosexuals Persecuted under Nazism, and by pressing one's face close to the small opening at its side, visitors can catch a glimpse of the dark interior. Seo Sookyung and I came across that park in the autumn of 2013 by chance, and saw the film that plays inside the cube, a film documenting the lives of sexual minorities who lost their lives under the Nazis. The upside-down triangles attached to their coat collars or sleeves were different from the Star of David, and at the time we thought they were of a dark colour because of the sepia or black-and-white colour of the film. Later we learned that this particular triangle had been used to brand people of certain sexualities and genders, and still later that queer men and women had been classified separately and assigned different triangles — one pink, the other black.

Type 'pink triangle' into a Korean search engine, and you're more likely to find images of women's briefs or woven fabrics with pink triangle patterning than images of the symbol the

Hwang 193

Nazis wielded so violently and has since become a symbol of activism, reclaimed pride, and struggles for human rights. Seo Sookyung and I had to scroll through reams of these before we found images of first the pink and then the black triangles we were looking for. The Nazis had forced gay men to wear pink triangles, thus branding them, but lesbian women were not assigned a separate badge; instead, they had to wear black triangles, the sign of what the Nazis classified as unsociable/asocial persons, or those who had unsanctioned sex, as in Aryans who slept with Jews. All this gave us pause. How might we interpret the fact that no stigmatising symbol existed for queer women? That there were less queer women than men? Or that they were less visible?

The 2,711 concrete slabs of the Holocaust Memorial are reminiscent of caskets of different heights and laid out in orderly rows over the entire site. It's as if one of these slabs had been hurled across the street to form the Memorial to Homosexuals Persecuted under Nazism, segregated from a group already segregated for the purposes of persecution and extermination, to stand askew and somewhat incongruously on the edge of a park. But where I read a repeating pattern of segregation and exclusion, Seo Sookyung saw singularity and visibility.

They had to do this to guarantee visibility, Seo Sookyung said. She added that the cube would have remained indistinct if it had been placed amid the densely packed memorial slabs on the Holocaust Memorial site, with the unintended consequence of obscuring the presence and fact of these people.

She had a point, as when we chanced upon the memorial we'd had no inkling of who it was commemorating, not until

194   *dd's Umbrella*

we'd seen its interior; nor had we been aware that queer people had been persecuted on such a massive scale during the Holocaust. Considering these facts, the location of the smaller memorial and the voyeuristic manner in which it invited participation seemed both relevant and incongruous, and yet it was this experience that stayed with us through our journey after we left Berlin and, much later and near the end of our trip, headed to Birkenau, sinking us into a spiral of bitter and solitary reflection.

Jung Jinwon was born the very year we visited those memorials. At five years old, their favourite colour is pink. After careful deliberation they will pick out the pink colour pencil, the pink jelly bean; when drawing anything or anyone they are particularly attached to, they always use pink. A year or two ago, Jinwon used to bestow pinkness on us as though it were an honour. I'm pink, they'd say. And when asked, What about Mama? they'd say, Mama is pink too. And Nini Thu-ggung (Sookyung)? Nini Thu-ggung is pink too. What about me? You... Okay, nini, you be pink too. (With a show of magnanimity.)

Jung Jinwon still adores pink, but after being bullied and intimidated by a kid in daycare for wearing pink socks, they've become reticent about expressing their preference. He said he would hit me if I wore pink socks again. Why is he mean to me? Why does he want to hit me?

P, the teacher at daycare overseeing Jinwon's care and education this year, doesn't use blue and pink as markers of gender, but recently, after telling Kim Sori about how Jinwon was bullied for sitting down to pee, did add: The thing is, even if that's what you've been doing at home with Jinwon, well...

the kids tease Jinwon, saying that's the girly way to pee, and, well, considering how hurtful those comments must be for Jinwon, perhaps it's a good idea to teach Jinwon to do as the other kids do? Thus fuelling our anxiety. The three of us were ready to trust P, who we rely on so much after all, and whose care work and labour allows us to manage our days, but even so, there are moments when we are forced to recognise that our trust in P may arise out of convenience rather than confidence. As when two girls from Grass Class held hands and walked over to P to say they were getting married and the teacher told them girls can't marry girls because girls are meant to marry boys according to common sense, and Jung Jinwon later repeated these words to us after seeing Seo Sookyung kiss my forehead.

8

Girls can't marry girls. Girls are meant to marry boys.

Oshii Mamoru's 2008 anime, *The Sky Crawlers*, opens with a dogfight involving three fighter jets. Tailed by a Kildren-piloted jet, the character known as Teacher performs an aerobatic manoeuvre that involves raising the nose to abruptly stall the plane and force the other jet to speed ahead, then assuming the six o'clock position to attack and successfully down his opponent. It was Seo Sookyung who told me this technique of getting on an enemy's tail is called Pugachev's Cobra manoeuvre. In a dogfight, having someone on your tail can be fatal and the Cobra can give you an advantage by putting you on the offensive, Seo Sookyung explained, but executing it is extremely difficult, not to mention hazardous, and fighter jets that allow the manoeuvre are extremely rare to begin with — usually it's a toss-up between the Russian multipurpose fighter jet Sur-37 or the American fighter Stealth F-22.

We saw *The Sky Crawlers* back when we lived in Yangcheongu. After some discussion we had decided to stay home for the summer — home being a single oktop room of half brick and half slate that was a poor defence against either the heat or the cold — and were flicking through satellite

198   dd's Umbrella

channels one day with tall iced lemon waters in hand when we happened to catch the film. Seo Sookyung had used fresh lemons to make our drinks, but they'd turned out too bitter, and the tall glasses sweated so much our palms dripped from holding them. We might have switched to another channel, but the sound of rapid breathing caught our attention as the screen opened up to wide skies.

The Sky Crawlers is a war story featuring innocent young fighters, and though the film turned out to be Japanese and Seo Sookyung and I couldn't be entirely partial to it, aware as we were of the war crimes committed by Japan during the Second World War, it affected us deeply nonetheless. We immediately purchased a Blu-ray of the film along with a Blu-ray player. The film is set in a world mired in ennui and unrest, a world that perpetuates 'authentic' war spectacles and the endless consumption of *Kirudore* (Kildren), who, as the liner notes to the Blu-ray of the film explains, are 'beings that have the outward form of adolescent girls and boys who neither grow, age, or die'. Trained as combat pilots, they cannot die except in battle. The Kirudore are mobilised in proxy wars to dispel social malaise. If in George Orwell's *Nineteen Eighty-Four* war is present as rumour and as propaganda about wars occurring elsewhere, in *The Sky Crawlers* it is present as entertainment in which lives are lost or saved right above people's heads, over the space of their daily lives. Kannami Yuichi, a Kirudore pilot, returns numerous times during these wars to his lover, Kusanagi Suito, who in turn waits for Kannami. In their waiting there is a readiness for and a concrete anticipation of death. This was what made such a deep impression on us.

I wait for you to return.

Seo Sookyung and I have lived together for twenty years now. Two decades ago, we found a small bedsit with a narrow fridge-less kitchenette, where we managed to fit in a desk, a shelf, and a chest of drawers. The room was a back-corner room and pitch black with the lights off at night. At the end of the day, I'd sit in the dark reading by the light of a desk lamp, periodically turning around to peer over at Seo Sookyung who would be sitting on the floor with her back against the wall, doing sudoku or reading. Seeing her face floating in her own small pool of light always gave me a deep sense of relief, and I'd either resume reading or go and snuggle beside her under the blankets. Now that we both earn a living, we're not as poor as we used to be in our teens and twenties. We each have a bed and a room of our own. When either one of us feels like talking or embracing or sitting together, we'll seek the other out for a long chat and either fall asleep together or return to our own rooms for the night. We are familiar with each other's objects and habits, gestures and sounds, but we do not take any of it for granted. Mornings waking each other up, the messages we exchange to check in on one another during the afternoons when we're working, the daily welcome awaiting us when we get home after a long day, weekends spent sleeping in and leisurely cooking lunch or dinner: these constitute our everyday, but we replay scenarios of how abruptly all this could end. I'll be on my morning commute or standing at a crossing waiting for the light to change after my lunch break, or waiting at home for Seo Sookyung, brushing my teeth in front of the mirror perhaps or preparing a light dinner for us to eat together, moments when I'm feeling tired and serene, or I'm quiet and not thinking of anything in particular — when suddenly, I'll fall. The sensation's usually fleeting and mostly

200 dd's Umbrella

passes if I focus on taking deep breaths, but not always. When it doesn't, I have to try my damnedest to believe that Seo Sookyung is, in that moment, safely out there in the world.

Were she to die, I would not even get a phone call.

I have never been free from this knowledge.

Twenty years of a life lived together but in an emergency, whatever has befallen one of us will not be communicated to the other. Were something life-threatening to happen to Seo Sookyung, the call will go to Seo Sookyung's family. If my life is ever threatened, the call will go to Kim Sori or my parents. And though there is some chance it may be otherwise, Seo Sookyung and I give more weight to the possibility that neither of us will get the call. We live with that possibility each day, always imagining each other's death and the moments leading up to that final moment. We experience loss in increments, as if we were swallowing poison. My daily prayer is for the safe return of Seo Sookyung. And every day Seo Sookyung returns home. From out there, from the daily threat of death, she returns home to me.

Give me a bone.

A bone?

In case you die first.

What good is a bone?

I want it as a keepsake.

Okay. You can have two if you want.

Don't you want one of mine?

Nah, I don't need one.

Why not? Why don't you want one of mine?

What good is it if you're already dead?

Still. Take one.

Alright.

We had a conversation like this once, but how likely is this really? Could we ask for each other's bones? Could I ask Seo Sookyung's family to share some of her remains with me? More to the point, what might our families demand of the remaining one of us?

On 20 October, 2013, in a neighbourhood in Bukgu, Busan, a woman in her sixties jumped from the rooftop of her building after her lifelong companion and partner died of cancer. But the reason the woman jumped was because she was about to be evicted from their home with nothing but the clothes on her back, the home she and her partner had lived in for over four decades as a result of her partner's so-called family exercising their legal rights. (Online news team, 'Friends from All-women High School Meet Tragic Death after "Living Together for 40 Years"', *Seoul Shinmun*, 31 Oct, 2013.) Coming across this news, Seo Sookyung and I had to confront the painful fact that this was one possible future for us. Seo Sookyung and I had bought our house in both our names, and we'd each written a will to say the deeds to the house would go to the remaining owner in the event one of us died before the other. We had made audio recordings of our wills as well. All to protect the life of whoever may remain, to protect us from each of our families. When it happened, would I or Seo Sookyung be able to live out the rest of our days in dignity and according to the wishes laid out in our wills?

We knew we should have our wills notarised to increase the chance they would be respected, and that we needed two witnesses to do so. Seo Sookyung and I are still waiting to find our two witnesses. Kim Sori could be one of the two. Could

202 dd's Umbrella

Jung Jinwon, once they're grown up, be the other witness? Will we one day explain our relationship to Jung Jinwon? What is our relationship? At hospitals, department stores, travel destinations, government offices, markets, and outside our front door, people ask us: What are you to one another?

What are we to one another?

We are, to one another, the person who waits to walk us home, the person who has welcomed us with joy every day for twenty years, the person who imagines a day when the other one will not make it home, the person who has promised to bear and witness the other's death at the closest proximity. We don't think everyone who asks about our relationship deserves an answer, but when we're asked, we always say we're friends or relatives. Not because this is the simplest and most convenient answer, but because it is the best way to protect ourselves from our neighbours. But even this isn't enough. We've already experienced what could potentially happen when our relationship is seen, when it becomes apparent.

Twenty years ago, the obscure backroom Seo Sookyung and I rented together for the first time was a first-floor room surrounded by walls. The two-storey house had been built in the 1970s and had separate entrances for the owners and tenants: a front gate and a side door practically located on opposite sides of the house, that's how far apart they were. But the man who was the owner of the house used to hang about the side door early in the morning or late at night, and brazenly ask us where we were going, what we were doing, or would say given how we were always together it sure looked like we were dating, like we had *that* sort of relationship. It was in that house that someone slashed the mosquito net outside our window one day, slashed it wide enough for a fist to fit through. The next time they slid our window open while we slept and left what looked like semen on the wall below. Then they started leaving a box of tissues on the wall outside our door every morning. The man spying on our private space morning and night and going to these lengths to jerk off could have been the owner of the house or could have been someone else, but the owner was the first person we suspected. Trying to think of who else it might be certainly didn't help with our anxiety. If it was him then there was only one perp, whereas if it wasn't, there could be any number of them. After experiencing firsthand how our relationship, simply for involving two women, could be the object of voyeurism, we avoided renting ground-floor or semi-basement rooms and lived in a constant state of vigilance, especially against sexual objectification and peeping Toms. As well as the array of potential words and deeds that our neighbours, realising the nature of our relationship, might potentially direct at us out of contempt for who we were.

What are you to one another?

I'd like to know: The neighbours who ask us this, do they really want the truth? What thoughts come before and after their idle curiosity, and do they count as thought? For instance when we are asked this question, Seo Sookyung and I must, regardless of whether we actually answer or not, consider the following: the threat we might encounter, whether together or separately, depending on our response; the potential ways our relationship with the interrogator might change as a result of our response; and the before and after, that is, the context of the initial curiosity and the consequences of answering to it.

204   dd's Umbrella

What of our neighbours though? Do *they* ever go through this level of consideration, reflection, and contextualisation? Or do they just blurt out the words?

No, unni. I remember Kim Sori saying. *No one's that interested in other people, and they certainly don't care enough about anyone else to be imagining such things.*

Because they don't need to think/know about other people.

*

Seo Sookyung, who is able to explain Pugachev's Cobra manoeuvre in terms of Bernoulli's equation and Euler's equation of motion, threw away the years of study and hard work that had taught her these principles, literally binned the books and materials and models and anything else to do with a maths degree and kept only a single round cast iron paperweight that had the university's name engraved on it, and this only because I was using it to weigh down the notes I had on my desk. Instead she chose to become a physical and rehabilitation therapist, and now she helps people who've had their plaster casts removed, patients recovering from cancer, and older people who've undergone muscle or joint surgery to regain strength and mobility. She also leads group physical sessions where people learn to strengthen weakened muscles. Some of the people Seo Sookyung meets through these classes try to find her a husband. 'There's this nice man I know who's still single.' 'He's young but has his own raw fish and seafood restaurant, and he's very hardworking. You fancy being the mistress of a seafood restaurant?' 'He's a university professor, he teaches Japanese.' 'The mother has a hundred million won saved up for her future daughter-in-law.' These proposals and one-sided conversations entirely disregard Seo Sookyung's two college degrees, and revolve solely on what the ideal marrying age 'according to common sense' is these days and how Seo Sookyung's already past it, how with each passing year her prospects will dwindle until she's left with men looking for their second wives, the wise thing therefore is to seize the opportunity that's presented itself, etc., in a persuasion tactic predicated on urgency and the need for haste.

Seo Sookyung usually laughs these comments away, being unconcerned by such talk, but the word *common sense* always gets me thinking — what do they mean, 'according to common sense'? What *is* common sense? Is it thought? When people mention common sense, don't they tend to equate it with their own opinions on a matter, and doesn't that then make common sense synonymous with thought? Even though, considering the word *sense*, it may be closer to a feeling or an impression towards the world. A sense that something is or should be a certain way.

In his notes to Hannah Arendt's *Eichmann in Jerusalem*, Hwa Yol Jung calls common sense 'a mode of thinking', and goes on to add that it is 'not only thought founded on the senses, it is also communal for it is held in common by all people' — so according to him common sense or *sensus communis* is, in fact, a form of thought. In which case, to extrapolate from his argument, isn't the 'common sense' applied to Seo Sookyung an innate common sense, not so much a mode of thinking but more an incapacity to think? And considering how by common sense we usually imply that something goes without *thinking*, it does seem that common sense is not quite thought...

206   dd's Umbrella

In all the situations where we declare something to be *just common sense*, how often are we, in fact, bypassing thinking and reasoning? Isn't it logical to say that common sense is more a firmly held conviction, an entrenched habit, than thought? How else are we to explain the sheer number of things we exclude any time we say, *that's just common sense*? That your common sense could be different from mine, that my claim of common sense might cause you harm isn't even considered here. In such instances common sense is neither sense nor thought, it's... Isn't it more a conventional determination, one that assumes that such-and-such a story will have such-and-such an ending while another such-and-such story will have another such-and-such ending?

When I share these thoughts, Seo Sookyung will gently tap my head and tell me I shouldn't let it bother me so, but it does bother me, it upsets me so much I feel like I should have a word with each and every one of them, I want to tell them how what one person calls common sense can reveal more of that person's unthinking aspect and how that sort of unthinkingness shows quite explicitly what kind of person they are; I want to say, just now, with those words, you were laid bare a little too explicitly. Laid bare, exposed, like the view of someone else's balcony seen through a clear window. Why is it we don't check in with ourselves the way we periodically declutter our balconies? Why not clear everything out and sort through each item, examine what's been piling up in there and dust and vacuum, clean the mildew away, mend or discard what's broken, reorganise and reorder everything... Why do we never bother to do this?

Is it because we don't need to?

9

We don't need to know.

I have a name for this type of attitude. I call it the world view of the mukja.

The Malling-Hansen typewriter Nietzsche purchased in 1882 as his eyesight was failing is unlike either the modern typewriter or the more familiar keyboards of today. The first time I saw an image of it, I was reminded of Pinhead in Clive Barker's *Hellraiser*. I figured Pinhead must have been inspired by the design of this freakishly beautiful object. The Malling-Hansen typewriter is a hemisphere studded with lettered keys that resemble oversized pins, and it's about the size of a man's skull, that of a northern-hemisphere white man such as Dieter Eberwein, perhaps, who has written about Nietzsche's typewriter. The human hands using this machine would have typed in a manner not unlike the gesture of hands caressing a head. This typewriter was called a writing ball. The Malling-Hansen writing ball was smaller and therefore more portable and also more affordable than a Remington typewriter, but commercially it fell behind the competition. Developed with American capital that had funded the manufacture of weapons as well as sewing machines, the Remington typewriter

208 dd's Umbrella

outmatched the writing ball in hardware improvements and distribution. The writing ball, however, was only available for purchase in Copenhagen. The manufacturer of the writing ball lacked the funds to open shops in the US or in Europe, nor could they afford to hire more personnel to fulfil higher production volumes and larger orders. The International Rasmus Malling-Hansen Society lists these reasons on their official website and goes so far as to state that money was the fundamental reason they lost the commercial competition. ('It is obvious that Malling-Hansen's invention couldn't win under these very unequal conditions, and the reason he lost the commercial competition should be obvious: lack of capital!')

Since learning about the writing ball, I've bemoaned the fact that most of today's typing instruments are not hemispherical in design. It's a real shame the writing ball didn't become the standard. How fitting and infinitely more beautiful it would have been for a machine that records human thought to have resembled a hemisphere! I imagine Nietzsche holding out his hands, fingers curled, to graze the writing ball as he tapped. I mimic the pose myself, imagining the tips of his fingers pattering away at the speed of thought... but Nietzsche never became skilled enough to use the writing ball for work. There seems to be several differing theories as to what held him back, but according to Dieter Eberwein, one of the vice presidents of the International Rasmus Malling-Hansen Society, it was likely because his machine was damaged during transport to Genoa. Nietzsche found a machinist to have it repaired, but the machinist was unaccustomed to the device and wound up causing more damage. And so Nietzsche's difficulties persisted.

Hwang 209

When a sighted writer begins to lose vision or becomes blind, how do they read and write?

How do they sense the sighted realm, which is the only world they've known?

Is the blind realm really as dark as it's been made out in written or verbal accounts? Is it as black as ink?

Some months ago, I was told 40 per cent of my optic nerve had atrophied and that it would continue to degrade and die. There would be no regeneration or recovery, what was lost would remain lost, and I was to prepare myself for further extensive loss. The doctor I spoke to was boyish and well-groomed. While he peered at the optic nerve through the vitreous body of my eyes using a special lens, I stared at the light emitted by his diagnostic instrument. It was orange and smelled of mint. The backrest on my chair was at such an angle that it thrust my body forward, and I had to tense my leg and back muscles through the examination to keep my upper body from collapsing. So what exactly is the problem? I asked. Is it intraocular pressure? No. I recently started using a smartphone, could that be why? No. Perhaps I read too much? No. Could it be my eating habits? I'm a picky eater. No. Is it from crying too much? No. This happens sometimes for no particular reason, the doctor answered shortly, then turned away to gaze at the test results on the screen. I looked to the corner where Seo Sookyung was waiting in one of the chairs set out for accompanying guardians. The lights were dimmed and I couldn't make out her expression. I asked the doctor to tell me what foods or activities I should avoid. He said there wasn't anything in particular, though I should avoid doing handstands. He prescribed some eye drops and said the treatment, as it were, for this condition was essentially in managing it, that the

210 dd's Umbrella

aim was to maintain my current condition and slow down further atrophy, to retain my central vision for as long as possible. With proper management you'll be fine, he said.

I distrusted his simple, no-fuss optimism. I still do. He said the condition had no observable symptoms, that I was unlikely to feel any pain, that despite everything at 1.0 my vision was still pretty good, and that none of this would seriously impact my daily life. And yet every time I try to focus my eyes on something now I feel dizzy and nauseous, and from time to time I'll feel a pain in my eyes, as if I have short needles bristling inside them. Then there's the perpetual headache from trying to look at things through unfocused eyes, and by evening I find it difficult to keep them open. But when I close my eyes, I see these tiny pops of lights, like the faintest dying trace of light particles the size of salt grains. And of course I'd gone to see him in the first place precisely because my daily life *was* impacted.

During the visit, I mentioned that I was a big reader and the doctor nodded and said that was fine, there wasn't much correlation between reading and optic nerve damage. No, I said, that's not what I mean. I'm always reading something, books or otherwise, and I noticed I don't see very well these days, the sentences are sometimes out of focus. Surely that's because when I look at something my eyes are seeing what's not visible first? The doctor cocked his head to one side. How does one see what's not visible? I don't know, but I see it, and that's what's causing all this discomfort, I said, but he kept cocking his head and repeating, I shouldn't think so, it shouldn't be a problem, you shouldn't be experiencing much discomfort. I stared at him, not understanding his words. Then I told myself he must have wanted, but had somehow omitted to add, *compared to more progressed cases.*

Hwang 211

What possibilities would remain when the sighted world ceased? What would one read and write with thereafter?

Would writing in braille with a slate and stylus be enough?

Was there enough literature transcribed into or written in the first place in braille? Enough to satisfy my desire to read, that is?

It was only after Seo Sookyung and I started asking these questions that we discovered that there was a term for the reading and writing system of sighted people — mukja, or ink script — just as the reading and writing system of blind people is called jeomja, or dot script. The fact that mukja was the language/instrument of sighted people, that notices on walls and signage and bulletins and announcements of various sorts, details and instructions and cautions and warnings on medicine bottle labels, not to mention this very sentence and every line in the various volumes and editions of Roland Barthes and Saint-Exupéry and Hannah Arendt and Raul Hilberg fell under this category, and that the *ability to see* all this was the basic premise of the world — all of this was something we only belatedly realised. Seo Sookyung and I wondered how we could have lived four whole decades without ever encountering the term mukja. In the vast sea of symbols that surrounded us, nearly all the languages those of us without sight loss or impairment ever came across were in mukja, not braille, yet we never knew there was an actual name for it. We never knew, learned, heard, read, or spoke about it, and the reason for this, as far as the two of us can make out, is, simply, that we never *needed* to say it.

It didn't need to be said.

The assumption of mukja but not braille as the normative standard, the normative state, is so widespread and so obviously

212 dd's Umbrella

constitutes what the sighted claim as common sense that we never needed to refer to it or call it by name.

I noticed something a few weeks after our first conversation about mukja. It was eleven o'clock on a Saturday morning, and I was at Yongsan Station waiting to board an ITX train. It was so cold my hands were numb inside my pockets. I saw a train pull in at the platform shared by the Gyeonggi/Gyeongui Central subway line and the Chuncheon-bound ITX train. A signal tone rang out to let people know the train was approaching, followed by an announcement: *The train is pulling into Platform 1…* I waited for the voice to state which train, but the announcement stopped there. The only information they'd thought to provide was that *a* train was arriving. I would have to figure out myself which train and where it was bound. Anyone unable to make out the text on the passenger information screen would be at a loss as to whether the approaching train was a subway train bound for Jipyeong or an ITX train bound for Chuncheon. Flustered, I looked up at the script spelling out Jipyeong on the screen. The train was bound for Jipyeong. But it seemed this was information that didn't require further communication, that didn't have to be conveyed through a spoken language. Nothing needed to be said.

Since anyone could see it.

That there might be someone at that particular hour on that particular day on that particular platform in that particular station not having access to mukja for whatever reason was a possibility that simply did not occur to the person who lived in the world of eleven o'clock on a Saturday morning, that is in the world of mukja. Or that such a person might be waiting on the platform without a companion. The one who saw didn't see the one who did not see. Why was someone who couldn't see standing there in the first place? And with that, such a person was dismissed, not taken into account, not counted. They were not a part of the landscape of common sense constructed there on that platform, at that station, in that moment, by people assuming sight and unimpaired vision, assuming uniformity. They were, simply, not there... I could still make out the text on the display screen and was therefore part of that landscape, I was in it, I *was* it, but one day I, too, would be erased. From the platform of mukja, from the supposedly uniform and unvarying common-sense world, yet again.

Is 'health' the underlying conceptual structure upholding that platform? According to common sense, I am not healthy. I'm not straight, I'll never be a good daughter, and I'm increasingly moving away from seeing without impairment. In the word *health* I smell oil adhering to steel, I sense pungent smoke fumes, and I see Nietzsche. Nietzsche first encountered the Malling-Hansen typewriter in 1882, the instrument that, however you look at it, resembles a human skull, and he not only completed part one of *Thus Spoke Zarathustra* in ten days in 1883, he went on to write *On the Genealogy of Morals*, which would be published much later in 1887, on that typewriter. During those four years, Germany's colonial enterprise began in earnest. If we consider as well the founding of Gesellschaft für Deutsche Kolonisation, the Society for German Colonisation, in 1884, Nietzsche's unravelling of *arya* as 'the "mighty", the "masters", the "holders of power"', his reference to 'shortness of the skull' in explaining the Goths in relation to *gut*/good and the logical leap in his claim that 'the subject race has finally again obtained the upper hand [...] in the

214   dd's Umbrella

intellectual and social qualities' were perhaps less the result of his own idiosyncratic thinking and more a reflection of the spirit of the times. In any case, Nietzsche wrote, and Nazism discovered in his writings a popular explanatory text that was profitable to its ends. I wonder if in the meantime his use of the Malling-Hansen typewriter influenced his phrenological pronouncements in any way. If a totalitarian world view sees humans as instrumental and co-opts them as a mechanical means to an end, couldn't we entertain the thought that some kind of instrument/skull-shaped typewriter may have been at the source of his claims? For *people are bound to speak and think according to the tools they have at hand...* I, who am not 'healthy' by any moral standard whether of Nietzsche's time or of my own time, open my copy of *On the Genealogy of Morals* and reread the one and only sentence in it that I truly want to return to and keep thinking about: 'We are unknown, we knowers, ourselves to ourselves'.

*

I would like to write a story called 'The Finish Line'.

Will I ever manage to finish it? I've been struggling for so long to write it.

A story in which no one dies.

I'll go on writing after I lose my sight. This I can type with my eyes closed: *I'll go on writing after I lose my sight.* The world of braille and touch will open up my other senses. I have faith. But can I have faith in my neighbours? *A blind woman lives here.* Would I start to fear going outside, start to prefer remaining indoors to hide my blindness because I do not trust my neighbours? Then there's the sheer waste: there are so many print books I still haven't gotten around to reading. And just as many that I need to reread several times over. I suppose I could always open up a book and touch the pages, but not being able to read what is written on those pages will be excruciating. Each page reverting to flat empty sheets against my fingertips. Will I still love them? The accrued silence of a million pages. Would I not wither away in the drought? Sometimes, as I hover in front of the bookshelf worrying myself with these thoughts, holding up my palm to cover first one eye then the other, Seo Sookyung will quietly walk over and place a hand on my head. I might ask her to read to me if my eyes hurt. We sit together side by side, reading and listening. I breathe in the smell of her neck and shoulder as I attend the sentences carried forth in Seo Sookyung's breath, I feel my body resonate with her reading voice which itself resonates, subtly and quietly, with the undulations of the story. Seo Sookyung reads well. The inevitability of this is something I realise all over again every time she reads to me. After all, she has yet to bore me as a narrator even after twenty years.

What if Seo Sookyung were to write the story?

What story would she write?

Would she be able to explain ourselves? To explain that today was today?

I'll have to wake everyone up in a minute.

Everyone is Seo Sookyung and Kim Sori and Jung Jinwon. They're all asleep, though it's past noon. We came over this morning to watch the news together over breakfast. Three years ago, we had planned to meet here too, to gather around this table with a chocolate cake for the child and a cream cake

216   dd's Umbrella

for the adults, a bouquet of ranunculus, and a few other gifts. Every year we get together on this day, and though what we bring to the table varies from year to year, it is a day of cakes and candles and flowers. And so, as usual, we'd planned a small party for the evening of 16 April, 2014. To mark Seo Sookyung's birthday.

10

In 2013 Seo Sookyung and I visited several European cities over a fortnight, ending our trip at Oświęcim, Poland. At Berlin Central Station we boarded a train that would take us over the border, changed to another train in Poznań, arrived late in the night in Warszawa, and took yet another train bound for Kraków the following day. From Kraków to Oświęcim we made the trip by bus, a cramped and dark minibus that departed from Kraków Central Bus Station. Outside the window, intermittent drizzle.

The docent at the first Auschwitz concentration camp was a woman who looked to be in her midfifties. She wore a two-piece skirt suit of matching colour, the jacket cinching her waist, and shoes with block heels under grey pantyhose. She led us to where the jars that once held ashes scraped from the crematorium incinerators stood, pointed at the numerals written there and told us that the number of the dead, the number of people sacrificed at Auschwitz was an estimate based on rough calculations, and that we still didn't know precisely how many had perished. *Uncountable.* We listened to her solemn, grave explanations as we toured the first camp, then boarded the bus and headed to the second camp.

218 dd's Umbrella

The gate at Birkenau was big enough for a train to pass through and the only means of entry into the place. When we arrived, we saw a group of young people with the blue-and-white Israeli flag draped about their shoulders walking over the tracks on that single route into the camp, their fists and voices raised like triumphant football players. (Were they the descendants of survivors? Were their shouts victorious returning cries signalling the triumph of life?) A docent guided us around the camp, the crematoria, and the pond where the ashes of women and children had been scattered. The last place we visited that day was the latrines. The docent pointed at a row of holes over which the prisoners had had to hurriedly lower their pants and crouch, then asked us if we knew what these holes signified. Looking at each of our hesitant, silent faces in turn, she answered her own question by saying the concentration and extermination camps were not intended as correctional facilities to imprison and reform, but were mechanical plants contrived to exterminate and dehumanise people. On our way out of the latrines someone asked the docent, in a mournful voice, what we were to make of how those who had experienced the Holocaust, that is the Israeli people, treated Palestinians, and the docent answered in an unyielding, solemn voice, We can't judge them.

I thought her words sounded like a mantra.

Well, think how often she's had to repeat that answer, Seo Sookyung said. So many of the visitors must ask that question, people from different parts of the world.

I guess, I said. I guess that's why she had a ready answer. *We can't judge them. We don't have the right.* A ready expression and tone from being asked the same question so many times — but doesn't that effectively make it a platitude, I wondered. How far was that answer from what Hannah Arendt called 'the lesson of the fearsome, word-and-thought-defying *banality of evil*'?

But these conversations and questions came later. During the actual visit, from the moment we boarded the bus that departed Auschwitz I and arrived at Auschwitz-Birkenau, Seo Sookyung and I had been unable to think or speak. We were overcome to the point that our throats were constricted, but this fear that gripped us wasn't from the horror of seeing the barracks for women prisoners, the latrines, the scratchings and nail marks left on the blackened walls of the gas chambers. It came from our realisation of the immensity of Birkenau. It was one vast field. There was no means of escape. People rounded up onto trains bound for these extermination camps would have, on arriving at Birkenau, been consumed by utter helplessness. What we've seen in films and documentaries about the Holocaust, the barbed-wire fences that actually surround the camps, were wholly unnecessary. The place itself, irrespective of its constituent parts, pronounced one consistent message: There is no escape.

*

On the evening of 16 April, 2015, Seo Sookyung's thirty-ninth birthday, we met in front of Daehanmun in Jeongdong, Junggu. Seo Sookyung was carrying a shapeless bag with a drawstring on her back. A red-and-green foldable foam seat that had flattened from use poked out of its mouth. Once the sun's down it's going to get chilly, Seo Sookyung said. We crossed over to the Plaza Hotel side, as direct access to Seoul Plaza was blocked by police buses encircling the plaza. Seo

220   dd's Umbrella

Sookyung and I walked past the wall of buses to the old City Hall building, where we found an opening. We'd arrived early, but there was already a large throng of people and it wasn't easy to make our way into the plaza.

When we eventually set foot on the grass, we were swept up in the surge. Everyone seemed to be on their phones saying, Where are you? I'm at such and such, I'll find you, come and meet me here. Seo Sookyung and I inched our way forward through the crowd, and after a few metres found a foothold on the front steps of the old City Hall building. Behind us, people who'd managed to find each other after numerous phone calls exchanged greetings above our heads. Seo Sookyung and I stood near them, in fact we were so densely packed together there was barely room to turn around, and we could hear every word as they exchanged pleasantries and news. We learned that most of them were old colleagues, and that one of them had brought a large bouquet of chrysanthemums and lilies to place before the children's photographs at the altar in Gwanghwamun once the memorial was over, but, they said, the bouquet had already lost some petals and was squashed from making it through the swarm of people. The flower shop they remembered had vanished, the voice said, it must have gone out of business and they'd had a hard time finding another one.

And how is your mother doing? The same person asked, and a man answered from behind my right shoulder in a relatively cheerful tone, Ah, well. He explained that his mother was awaiting an operation to treat her chronic hip pain, but that he and his brothers weren't convinced she should have the surgery. His mother had undergone knee surgery ten years ago, and pain had made postsurgical rehab difficult even then, and, well, a hip operation was a different thing altogether, it required prolonged bed rest even before rehab, and the family worried that their elderly mother, whose condition could go from bad to worse on any given day, might not recover her strength after a long bout of bed rest, and though the surgery may well lessen the pain, he worried about the risk of her not being able to walk afterwards. Quality of life, that was his main concern, he said.

I was standing with my head slightly bowed so as not to squash the bouquet behind me, but after a while the stiffness in my neck got to be too much. Seo Sookyung squeezed my shoulder and swapped places with me. Neither of us had eaten that afternoon. Seo Sookyung rummaged in her pockets and found a nut bar. We split it between us, then looked at the stage installed on the plaza in the direction of Mugyo-ro. The stage was brightly lit but too distant for us to make out the people on it. Still, we stood facing it. It was 16 April, 2015, but the Sewol ferry remained at the bottom of Maenggol Channel and nine people were still missing.

The blue-and-white model ship on stage started to rise up. Everyone fell silent. A hush blanketed the entire plaza. It was the three-hundred-and-sixty-sixth day since the MV Sewol, operated by the Chonghaejin Marine Company, had capsized and sank off Jindo Island. The sun was down; night set in.

A few people were handing out chrysanthemums. We each received one and headed towards Gwanghwamun. The streetlights had come on. Sejong-daero echoed with footsteps. As we approached Cheonggye Plaza, the flow of people slowed and grew compact. At Cheonggye Plaza intersection it stopped entirely. Seo Sookyung and I moved out of the road and onto

222   dd's Umbrella

the pavement as a few others were doing. We got on tiptoe to
see what was happening up ahead. The police had erected a car
wall fronted by a police cordon to block Sejong-daero, making
Gwanghwamun Square inaccessible. People near the car wall
were shouting for the road to be opened. It hadn't rained but
the ground was wet, and the air smelled of capsaicin.
Somebody said entry to the subway station was barred. They're
blocking it so we can't even access the underground walkway.
From somewhere behind the car wall someone began intoning
the Miranda warning through a megaphone. Seo Sookyung
stood still and listened, then said the voice had just declared:
You have the right to say anything that can be used against you.
What? I said. They said you have the right to say anything that
can be used against you, not you have the right *not* to say
anything that can be used against you. I looked up to see who
was talking, but none of the police officers standing high up on
the other side of the car wall staring down at us was holding a
megaphone. The voice said for the second time: You have the
right to say anything, anything that can be used against you.
The police have the right, according to Article 37 of the
Constitution... to apprehend you in flagrante delicto, we
advise you to disperse immediately for your own safety... Seo
Sookyung saw that her chrysanthemum stem was broken and
twisted off the drooping neck, casting it to the ground. My
flower was smaller and, so far, faring better. We followed the
crowd as it moved towards Cheonggyecheon to find a different
route into Gwanghwamun, holding on to our
chrysanthemums.

The pavements either side of Cheonggyecheon were
narrow, and the row of police buses lining the street made the
pavements seem even more cramped. We pushed ahead in the

press of people through that narrow passage, peering up at the night sky. Seo Sookyung said there was something off about tonight, and I agreed. We gazed up at the night sky glittering with city lights, until we realised the strangeness was due to the stillness around us. It was a Thursday night but the usual glut of sounds that fill Gwanghwamun and Jongno were gone. The whooshing of cars speeding past, all the usual noises heard in the city centre around that time of day were absent, there was only the hum of people talking among themselves or chanting these words as they walked along Cheonggyecheon:

Scrap the Sewol Bill.

Scrap the Sewol Bill.

Step Down Park Geun-hye.

Salvage Sewol Ferry Now.

Seo Sookyung and I looked for a way out of Cheonggyecheon-ro, and at some point, though neither of us has a clear memory of the moment, found a narrow alley and made our way out to Jongno. There it was in front of us, with an abruptness that seemed unreal. We found groups of people here too. We couldn't tell which of the people walking ahead or behind or alongside us were the people we'd walked alongside in Cheonggyecheon, nor could we tell which of them were on their way to Gwanghwamun Square or to the nearby cinema. One or two police officers stood in the middle of the road, whistles in their mouths. The police had diverted traffic and most lanes were empty, but no one seemed to notice, and no one was choosing to step into the road to avoid the crowded pavements. Seo Sookyung and I slowly wound our way through the pedestrians, hearing snatches of conversation as people looked for a coffee spot or shopped for

224   dd's Umbrella

spring clothes. Past Jonggak, the street suddenly emptied. Seo Sookyung and I stepped down onto the road to avoid the phalanx of shield-carrying police waiting to mobilise and continued walking until we finally arrived at the intersection at Sejong-daero. The area was entirely blocked off by police buses. We realised the car wall we'd seen from Cheonggye Plaza was in fact layered. Sejong-daero, which stretches from north to south, was severed at its waist by a double layer of car walls, and we couldn't access it in either direction. We could see over the two walls that the wide boulevard had been completely emptied of cars and pedestrians. The intersection had become its own contained space, a void between two long expanses of wall. A loud cry rose up from the crowd that remained on the southern Cheonggye Plaza side of the wall. It seemed a substantial number of people still remained there. Now what do we do? we asked each other.

Shall we continue on?

We walked westward in the direction of Seodaemun and entered a side street past Kumho Art Hall. Compared to the boulevard, the air in the street behind Sejong Center for the Performing Arts had more of a bite, and the ginkgo branches emitted a pale green light with the newly sprouted leaves of spring. Seo Sookyung said she couldn't remember if Kannami Yuichi says *teacher* or *father* in the very last dogfight as he flies after the other plane and asked me if I did.

You mean in *The Sky Crawlers*?

Yeah, what is the last thing Kannami Yuichi says? *I'll kill my father* or *I'll kill my teacher*?

Father, I said. It was unexpected, I remember being surprised. In *The Sky Crawlers*, Teacher is the mysterious pilot of the fighter plane marked with a black panther, an undefeatable pilot whose identity is unknown. The world of *The Sky Crawlers* maintains a precarious balance of peace and ennui through endless proxy wars between Lautern and Rostock. Any time one of these two companies exceeds the other in fighting power and threatens the balance, Teacher appears to restore it. None of the Kirudore pilots, including Kannami Yuichi, can defeat Teacher. That is the fixed script of that particular world, system, entertainment. The eternal children are unable to triumph over Teacher/Father, and their battle/ death is unending. That is the default. Realising this, the Kannami Yuichi of a previous life is plagued by a sense of futility and eventually kills himself, whereas the Kannami Yuichi of this life goes back to kill Teacher. Knowing the odds of him beating Teacher are minimal, he accepts the challenge nonetheless, and surely the reason he fights back despite the low odds is because there's no escape, don't you think? Seo Sookyung asked. In a world where breaking free is an impossibility, the pilot has no other option but to return and kill Father/Teacher/the default. If escape is out of the question, then one has to take flight here, one has to risk friction *here*.

Tal-Joseon, Seo Sookyung said. The people who say they want to leave this country, escape this hellish anachronistic place — but if they were to leave, where would they go?

We followed the side street between the Annex Government Complex and Sejong Center and reached the northern section of Sejong-daero. Seo Sookyung headed for Gwanghwamun Square, walking right across the emptied lanes of the boulevard. I followed behind. However and whichever way they'd come, a long line of mourners were already assembled on the square, carrying candles as they waited to pay

226   dd's Umbrella

their respects at the altar set up in the heart of Gwanghwamun. Kyobo Building to the east, clouds speeding towards the moon, the north- and south-bound lanes of Sejong-daero on either side, the headquarters of Choson Ilbo to the southwest: all were visible at a glance from the public square.

*

On 16 April, 2016, we made our way up to Gwanghwamun Square via the underground walkway and subway entrance. The forecast had warned of bad weather, and we both wore our winter coats with the down liners removed. Before we walked out to the square we slipped on rain ponchos over our coats. It was raining, and the rain soon turned torrential. The ponchos wouldn't close over our bulky coats and rucksacks. Seo Sookyung and I tried to help each other with the buttons, then resigned ourselves to leaving a couple of buttons undone. We took our foam seats out. People ahead opened their umbrellas but the people behind asked that they be folded away. The umbrellas disappeared to reveal backs and heads covered in raincoats and plastic ponchos. The ground was slick with puddles and rainwater, and the rain lanced down and splattered more water. The rain gear seemed pointless. Rain lashed at our chins. Someone with a microphone asked people to please sit down in consideration of the people in the back. In the police-cordoned space to one side of Gwanghwamun Square, a space that was smaller than usual because fewer people had come out than in the previous two years, we took our seats. The water started to seep in.

11

On 20 January, 2009, evicted residents and shopkeepers protesting the demolition of the Namildang Building on Hangangno-2-ga in Yongsangu were kettled onto its rooftop, isolated, and killed. These events reminded me of what Seo Sookyung and I had experienced in 1996 at Yonsei University: the barricade erected inside the building, the isolation, the fire. As we watched news footage of the lookout tower the protestors had set up on the roof engulfed in flames, Seo Sookyung and I said nothing but knew exactly what the other was thinking. *That could have been us.* Not that we've returned to the Namildang site since. What good would that do? It would only confirm our own powerlessness. And we weren't... we weren't the ones being evicted. We weren't, we aren't, we never would be subject to eviction. At least that's what we believed.

Between 9.26 and 9.38 a.m. on 16 April, 2014, as the Coast Guard's CN-235 patrol aircraft, B-511, B-512, B-513 helicopters and Coast Guard Vessel 123 arrived off East Geocha Island and began circling the capsized Sewol ferry with no attempt to radio the crew ('Coast Guard's Vessel 123, patrol aircraft CN-235 and helicopters made zero attempts to communicate with MV Sewol during the sinking', People's Commission for the Truth of the

228 · dd's Umbrella

Sewol Ferry Sinking, *Sewol Ferry Sinking Fact Check: What We Know So Far and What Remains to Be Revealed*, Book Comma, 2017.) —

When it was confirmed only after 12.00 p.m. that earlier reports claiming everyone on board had been rescued were false and that passengers remained aboard the sinking ship —

When we lost all words watching the ship's upended keel —

In these moments the thought *that could have been us* or *but we're not them* didn't even cross our minds.

The boat went on sinking and all we could do was stay with it, as witnesses and bystanders.

After 16 April, 2014, Kim Sori stopped coming over. Seo Sookyung and I didn't visit her either, though we lived maybe a hundred metres and a ten-minute leisurely walk away. Jung Jinwon was a baby then, which made outings difficult, and I still wonder how Kim Sori managed to fill up the days during that period.

I don't remember exactly when we started seeing each other again. It may have been around mid-May. We had dinner together. We talked about this and that: colleagues, Jung Jinwon's schooling, our concerns. I don't recall all of what we discussed over the subsequent months, but I do know we barely mentioned the Sewol sinking. We talked about everything but that. If the subject ever came up, it was only in passing, a few mumbled words here and there amid all our jokes, idle talk, worries, promises, confirmations, and many conversations. What we'd witnessed and what we were thinking, Kim Sori and I never confessed to the other. But though we evaded the issue, we still found ourselves circling back to it at times while talking of other things. Then we would trail off and either change the subject or fall silent. Kim

Sori knew that Seo Sookyung and I followed every new development in relation to Sewol ferry and the ongoing vigils and protests, that we had made this a focal part of our life. The two of us each had rucksacks packed with snacks and towels and foam seats always at the ready, and on weekends when there was a protest or a vigil for Sewol ferry, we headed to the square or to the streets with these slung over our shoulders. Seo Sookyung refrained from talking about the next scheduled gathering to Kim Sori. I think she worried that even the mention of it might burden Kim Sori, especially as Sori had a child herself. I worried too. Because she had a child. And because I was afraid. Afraid that she might tell me to stop.

Can't you give it a rest, unni?

I dreaded the moment she might say this to me, which meant that when she finally did, I had a biting comment at the ready. It was 16 April, 2016, and Seo Sookyung and I had come home from Gwanghwamun Square dripping with rain. We were grumbling about how we couldn't stop coughing, how heavy the rain had been, and how powerless we were starting to feel at the protests.

Can't you give it a rest, unni? Kim Sori said.

Give what a rest?

Talking about all that.

It's not like I've been talking about it a whole lot though, is it?

Yeah, you are, all the time. Even when you're not, you are.

And what if I am? Are we not allowed to? Is that why you never say a word about it?

Kim Sori gazed at me quietly then and said she was simply unable to talk about it. She said I had no idea what it was like to have a growing child at home. To see how slowly and how

230 *dd's Umbrella*

quickly a child grows, you've no idea, unni, she said. Parents who share the same space witness the trails left by their child every single day, she said. To live with a child is to be swept up in an endless whirlwind of emotions and to notice all the markers of their existence. Take our place: it's full of toys stuffed into odd places, all manner of chewed-up objects, nappy clothes, picture books left open, drawings and doodles. Every time I come across these traces of life, I think about the children on that ferry. Of the mothers and fathers who would have witnessed and stumbled across these daily reminders until their children reached the age they were. So don't talk to me as if I have to think about that day. I think about it. I think about their homes, about the people in them. That's why I can't talk about it. It scares me.

Why? Why does it scare you?

It just does.

What do you have to be scared about? Are you afraid of what you might feel if you talk about it? Is that it?

Kim Sori didn't answer.

That's your biggest fear?

On 26 November, 2016, as I waited my turn in front of the restrooms that connected to the underground Haechi Madang leading up to Gwanghwamun Square, that last question came back to me. Why had I responded like that? My question had been a thinly veiled accusation, I had effectively called her a coward, even if I'd couched my words for fear I might say something irrevocable. Maybe I'd wanted or needed to say those words back then, to accuse anyone or anything of cowardice, and it hadn't mattered whom or what I was accusing. What did Kim Sori make of me that day? Did she find me cruel and unfeeling? Would she have thought I was being mean? Or cowardly? Seo Sookyung had intervened at that point to calm us down — Kim Sori and I were glaring at each other, our faces pale with emotion — and make sure the situation didn't get out of hand. I'd expected Sori to leave in a huff and not return for a few days, but she stayed and had tea then returned the next day and the next for dinner. Afterwards, we pretended as if the entire conversation and especially the argument had never happened, but I knew that each of us carried the memory of it still and would go on remembering for a good long while. I supposed that we would, one day, speak of it. Would I be able to apologise to her then, I wondered.

I was deep in my thoughts when I heard a voice say, I couldn't care less about protests but it's all getting to be too much, and the more I think about it, it just doesn't seem right. Some women standing ahead of me in line were talking. They didn't appear to know one another. I gleaned that they lived in different areas and had arrived at the square at different times. One woman in a short-brimmed wool hat said she had been there since midday. She added that she hadn't missed a single rally so far — this was the fifth candlelight protest demanding the president's impeachment — and that she should be awarded for perfect attendance. Another woman, who was wearing an appliqué jacket and had a thick muffler wound around the entire lower half of her face, said she arrived an hour and a half ago and that this was her first time at the protest. A third woman who had not one but two PARK GEUN-HYE OUT stickers attached to her coat said she'd arrived a bit earlier than the second woman and that this was her third time. I mean, I

232   dd's Umbrella

don't know a thing about demos, she said, I've steered clear all my life, but I got so fed-up following what they'd done on TV, it's all so dirty and corrupt and I couldn't bear to sit and watch anymore. I mean, she's the *daughter*... What are you talking about? someone else asked as the woman trailed off. You didn't know? They say there's even video — and my husband, who's been such a big supporter, *he* said there's no letting things lie now, he was adamant... Let's see how it pans out, I'd thought, let's wait and see, wait and see, but no, this is plain wrong! That's why I'm here now, with my son and all in tow...

26 November, 2016: a month after cable channel JTBC's Newsroom aired a special on the files found on a tablet once owned by Choi Soon-sil — the unelected power, as it transpired, behind Park's Cheongwadae — and the fifth day of protests demanding that the president take responsibility for such a flagrant manipulation of state affairs, and that the National Assembly impeach her. Pundits had anticipated a relatively small crowd given the snowy weather, but in Seoul alone 1.5 million people gathered in the square. (Lee Seung-hyeon, '1.5 Million-strong Candlelight Protest, Zero Arrests... Peace Trumps Rage', *Edaily*, 26 Nov, 2016.) I'd said yes when Kim Sori asked if we were going to the rally again this week, but Seo Sookyung and I had, in fact, been thinking we would skip this one. We were tired. We couldn't bear the thought of having to sit for hours on the cold hard ground again. No matter how warmly we bundled up, by the time we headed home the chill was in our bones and we couldn't stop shivering. It took us a couple of days or more to shake off the chill each time, and we had been taking cold medicine for several weeks by now. Another headache at these protests was trying to find, or reach,

a restroom, as the crowds got so big it was impossible to walk through them mid-rally. Most of all, there was no way to avoid being in uncomfortable proximity to other people as we entered or exited the square, and involuntary physical contact was something both of us had a low tolerance for under the best of circumstances. At the square our cheeks, chests, stomachs, backs, glutes, calves... even our heels would brush up against strangers, and we moved or were moved as if carried along by the press of bodies, our faces silent and frowning all the while, until we finally reached the edge. There we'd have to find a corner where we could stand and wait for the unpleasantness and vertigo to subside.

The pervasive tone of these rallies, that is the emphasis on their peaceful quality, was something I discovered didn't sit well with me either. The insistence on peaceful protests seemed to verge on a compulsion in our eyes. We found the pride people seemed to take in being good citizens and peaceful protestors, an attitude that was occasionally visible in the square or in spaces where public opinion gathered, *unsettling*. Was this how sanctioned protests by good orderly citizens were categorically set apart from unsanctioned deviant protests by the not-so-good citizens? Did it imply that the families of the victims of the Sewol ferry sinking including the victims whose bodies were yet to be recovered had, for the last three years, not been good citizens? Just the day before, some farmers driving their tractors up to Seoul in protest had had their tractors confiscated by police and their heads beaten in (Han Woojoon, 'Police Erect "Car Wall" at Entrance of Anseong IC, Block Seoul-bound Jeon Bong-joon Fighters', *Korea Agriculture News*, 25 Nov, 2016.), but on this day, I knew the stickers would reappear in Gwanghwamun, the bloody flower stickers... (Kang Shin, Hong Inki, & Kim Heeri,

234 dd's Umbrella

'"Turn the car wall into a flower wall": Protestors Bring Easy-peel Flower Stickers to Facilitate Clean-up Duty of Drafted Police', *Seoul Shinmun*, 26 Nov, 2016.) Muttering under my breath, I packed up my rucksack again with my protest kit and a few snacks, then sat on the subway with the bag in my arms, complaining until the moment we reached Gwanghwamun that today of all days I really did not want to attend. If it weren't for the snow or the cold, if we weren't worried that not enough people would show up because of the weather, I would have stayed home. But when we got to the square people were out in droves, there were definitely more people there than in the previous week.

I washed my hands at the sink and headed back out towards Haechi Madang, passing what seemed an interminably long line of people by the toilet entrance. I walked up the gentle incline that led to Gwanghwamun Square. Seo Sookyung was waiting at a spot about fifty metres north of the King Sejong statue. The thought of having to weave a treacherous course through all the seated people filling up the square, twisting this way and that to find a toehold, filled me with dread. It had stopped snowing, but the temperature was bound to fall even more. Retying my loosened scarf, I started towards Sejong Center, then noticed a man holding a sign to his chest. On the A4-size sign, five character-letters were printed in plain type:

惡女 OUT.

EVIL BITCH OUT.

The man noticed me staring at him and moved the sign up to hide his face.

The waves began.

Seo Sookyung and I raised our candles then lowered them. The wave rolled on behind us. The crowd was said to stretch all the way back to City Hall and Seosomun-ro, it was bound to take a while for the wave to reach the fringes. I turned and watched the wave roll away until I couldn't make it out anymore. How many people were here? Who were they all? They were probably too diverse to categorise as one 'all'. Yunghee, Soonhee, Cheolsu, Geumju, Okja, Jongjin, Geumhee, Sejin, Seohee, Taeyoung, Kyeongshin, all these names had to be out there in the sea of people... As well as the resident of the apartment complex near us who for weeks now had had a banner tacked up on their living room window demanding the president step down. Perhaps even 'fifth male heir, third eldest son' T was in the crowd, and the woman in Seo Sookyung's group class who upon belatedly hearing of Sam Smith coming out as nonbinary had ranted about how scandalised she was and how her pastor always says *people like that, fiery depths of hell...* Seo Sookyung unwrapped a sweet and put it in my mouth, then grabbed my hand with her free hand. She had her hood up to block the wind, and from under it her nose and lips peeked out, both red with cold. From behind us, the wave rolled back accompanied by a thunderous roar. Seo Sookyung and I raised our candles and brought them down again. I told Seo Sookyung about the *evil bitch* sign I saw on the way back from the toilets. How the *woman* character alone, 女, was written in red.

How insufferable, Seo Sookyung said. It was, I said, insufferable and also unsettling. Because... Well, because the person who has to see that sign isn't the president, who's tucked away in the depths of Cheongwadae, but *me*. I'm the bitch-woman. If 惡女 OUT is that man's language of choice in this moment, then that is his tool, but does he even realise how his tool impacted me just now, what it did to me? Why can't

236 dd's Umbrella

he see the scores of women who've come out here today, same as him? Why can't he see them as clearly and vividly as he sees the womanhood of the person he's referring to in his sign, so explicitly as 惡女 and in vivid red too? Looking at that sign, I wanted to give him a piece of my mind, wanted to tell him don't do this, don't use words in this way...

And did you?

I wasn't sure if I should, something kept stopping me, I said. Since we're supposed to be a *we* here and now... A part of me was reluctant to create trouble when everyone has come here out of goodwill and to achieve a common goal. In the end I said nothing, but I know this is going to keep me up when we get home. I know I'll be haunted by my failure to say something, and by the terrible lie, the big, unbearable illusion that *we* implies unity.

The candle wax dripped onto my wool glove. I removed the glove, which by now was glued to the candle, quickly realised my hand preferred its warm, wax-coated interior over the freezing air, and wriggled it back on. There were candle drippings on my rucksack. I started scratching at the fabric, and the woman sitting next to me leaned in to tell me that wasn't the way to remove candle wax. If I were you, she said, I'd leave the drippings until I go home, then use an iron and a clean white sheet of paper. She was explaining how best to do this to Seo Sookyung and me when another wave surged towards us from behind.

*

On 3 December, 2016, after an arduous process, the National Assembly introduced a bill to impeach the president. (Song

Sookyeong & Seo Hyerim, '171 National Assembly Members of "The 3 Opposition Parties & Independents" Propose Bill to Impeach President Park', *Yonhap News*, 3 Dec, 2016.) The crowds gathered in the public squares were angry. 1.7 million people in Seoul and 2.32 million people nationwide took to the streets with candles. (Lee Sangyeop, '"Unbelievable"... 2.32 Million Candles Nationwide, Sets New Record Again', *JTBC*, 4 Dec, 2016.) It was also the day 416 torches were carried from Gwanghwamun to Cheongwadae, to within a hundred metres of its entrance. (Choi Gayoung, 'The Tragic Significance of the "Number" of Torches Headed to Cheongwadae', *YTN*, 4 Dec, 2016.)

Seo Sookyung and I walked behind the crowd shouting, Step Down Now, Disband Saenuri Party. We marched past Gwanghwamun and headed north towards Jahamun-ro to arrive outside the Cheong-woon and Hyojadong Community Center. People sat in the road and people were taking turns to speak into a microphone. Workers from Cort Guitars (Cor-Tek Corporation) and Yoosung Enterprise, residents of Seongju County protesting the deployment of a US THAAD anti-missile defence unit were some of those who spoke. There are so many issues I'd had no idea about, said one speaker, but coming here and meeting people directly involved in the various struggles and listening to their stories has been the biggest thing I've learned at these rallies. As the person spoke, someone decided to light a firecracker. Sparks shot up into the air one after the other, *pop-pop-pop* right above the heads of people seated on the side of the road. People looked about anxiously. Put it out, a few muttered. The man in the wool coat who had lit the firecracker turned round, looking sheepish, and shook his head at the crowd, saying once it was lit there was nothing he could do to turn it off, he had to wait

238 dd's Umbrella

until it was spent. The sparks continued lighting up the night sky as people sat and waited in tense silence.

Seo Sookyung and I sat in silence alongside them in the surrounding hush, and saw, in the crowd's wish for the protest to remain peaceful, their wounds. Perhaps what they wanted was to say, *We've seen people get hurt more times than we can count. Let's make sure no one else is hurt. We've been through enough.*

On Friday, 9 December, 2016, the impeachment bill was voted through the National Assembly (Lee Seung-gwan & Hyeon Hyeran, 'National Assembly for Impeachment of President Park... 234 Vote Yes, 56 Vote No', *Yonhap News*, 9 Dec, 2016.) and submitted to the Constitutional Court for a ruling. The very next day, which was a Saturday, Seo Sookyung and I took the subway to Seodaemun Station and started walking towards Gwanghwamun.

The surge began.

12

How will today be remembered?

On an afternoon in September 1939, a few days after the Second World War broke out, Stefan Zweig went on a walk 'for a last look at peace', and on his way back noticed his own shadow before him. In *The World of Yesterday*, he likens this to '[seeing] the shadow of the last war behind this one', but goes on to add that 'every shadow is also the child of light,' and it is on this note that he ends the book. Nonetheless, when the United States joined the war following Japan's attack on Pearl Harbor, he was convinced the world was headed to its tragic demise and, in February 1942, committed suicide with his partner Lotte Altmann. 1 September, 1939: Nazi Germany invades Poland. 7 December, 1941: Japan attacks Pearl Harbor. 8 December, 1941: US declares war on Japan. 22 February, 1942: the deaths of Lotte Altmann and Stefan Zweig. And the day before 22 February, 1942. These are the dates that once comprised Zweig's today.

On the last page of *The World of Yesterday*, there is a photograph of the Zweig couple. In it the two lie side by side on a bed. The bedding looks comfortable, and on the bedside table there is an oil lamp, a bottle of alcohol, a matchbox, and what I presume are coins. The two are leaning against one

240 dd's Umbrella

another, seemingly deep in slumber. Had someone sneaked into their room while they slept to take this photograph? But there are hints that lead us to surmise that the couple were already dead when the photograph was taken: Zweig wears a tie, and on Lotte's chin, which lies on his shoulder, there's a stain of what appears to be vomit. Today cannot shake off the shadow of the past, and these two sought to escape, wholly, from that shadow, from their today. Stefan Zweig and Lotte Altmann had both been through a war already; for them 1942 and the world to come likely seemed a concrete, self-evident reality. The 'war of all against all' that had started up once again, the persecutions, the deportations, the obliteration of the human spirit, all of it all over again. For them, today was without doubt today, a day that could not be other than what it presently was, that held no promise of a new, different day.

I close the book and glance up at the clock. Twenty-three minutes past one.

A dream catcher hangs below the clock.

The size of a human palm, its wispy grey-white branches are as light as bird bones and have been bent to form a round frame woven together by a mesh of fishing line and colourful threads. We came across it years ago on an overnight trip to an island, in the small workshop where we spent the night. There was a sign announcing the sale of cigarettes in one corner of the room, although one of the letters was missing. The room resembled a storage space in the midst of a chaotic emptying-out rather than a lodging or an artisan's workshop. But there were several dream catchers hanging throughout the space. They were all made by the owner. She described them as nets that scoop out bad dreams, and when we showed an interest she began to tell us how she'd crafted each one in a simultaneously nonchalant and pleased manner. All of them were made with what had once been trash: plastic, glass, fishing lines, nets. She collected the debris that washed up along the shore and left them to dry out over several weeks. The branches used to make the frames too were driftwood the tides had carried onto the shore: wood that had dipped and risen and dipped and risen, over and over for a long time, and that was sturdier for it and insusceptible to rot... That's how she described it anyway as she sold me our dream catcher. The house she had inherited from her grandmother was much too close to the sea. I remember her pointing out the traces left by the tides the previous summer on its walls and telling us the sea was encroaching on the house every year. It's been well over a decade since our visit. I wonder how her house has fared in that time.

A net that scoops out bad dreams.

I find it increasingly difficult to make out the state of the dream catcher. The irregular pattern of its net appears blurred in some places while remaining clear in others, like something seen through a glass pane beaded with water, making it difficult for me to appreciate it whole. I'll never see its overall mesh pattern as distinctly as I used to. I take a deep breath in and notice how the grey feather on the farthest edge of the dream catcher sways lightly as I breathe out. For the last ten years we've sat under this feather, this dream net, at this table, talking about everything that interests and enrages us, and this is where we gathered again this morning.

10 March, 2017.

How will today be remembered?

242 *dd's Umbrella*

Today the Constitutional Court unanimously upheld the National Assembly's December 2016 vote to impeach the 18th President of the Republic of Korea, Park Geun-hye.

How will people remember this day?

If she's impeached, then the revolution will be complete, some argued. The Donghak Peasant Revolution of 1894-95, the People's Congress Movement of 1898, the April 19 Revolution of 1960, the June 1987 Democracy Movement — all would be complete, all would be won. We would finally be on the winning side of history when we had never, not really, not ever, *won*. We would be the first generation in the entire modern history of this country to experience triumph, they said. And what a precious, overwhelmingly inspiring, historical experience it will be for all those who have filled the streets in hopes of the president's impeachment, not to mention...

Well, yes. It will be for me too. *To live is to receive the forms of the life of the sentences that preexist us*, as Barthes said, and after spending an entire season collectively writing new sentences, people are declaring that the definitive sentence has finally been written. So is today that day? The day the revolution is completed? Have we really achieved revolution, at long last and without bloodshed?

Kim Sori called me last night to ask if the two of us would come over to her place today instead of heading to Gwanghwamun. She wasn't sure she could bear to watch the impeachment trial on her own, she said. That's why we gathered here this morning. The televised ruling began at 11.00 a.m. and was over by 11.21 a.m. Everyone in Gwanghwamun Square and outside the Constitutional Court would have heard the ruling. The moment the decision to remove the President from office was read out, the square would have exploded in a tumult of cheer and elation. A festival of triumph and completion. The morning air was nippy but no one would have noticed, or they wouldn't have cared. Maybe a wave surged through the crowd, like it had the previous night. People would have raised their arms as if they were toasting one another, and the wave would have rippled from end to end, from street to street, on and on and on, and then... I imagine the wave subsiding and leaving this table in its wake. I see us, the ones slumbering here, seated round it, under our small net of dreams.

It's time to wake everyone up.

Even as I'm waking them up I'll be wondering if the revolution is possible here. *It happened, therefore it can happen again.* (22 September, 2017, at the Sewol Ferry Academy. Park Rae-gun, co-chairperson of the 416 Network, quoting Primo Levi's words from *The Drowned and the Saved*.) Could this phrase apply here? Could the story of this place be a story of revolution?

I close the books and stack them to one side of the table. Osip Mandelstam's *There Is Nothing that Needs to Be Said* is at the bottom of the stack. What could have prompted the editor to choose that line as the title of the whole collection? ('Where Mandelstam's poems are untitled, the first line stands as the title', 'Editor's Note' in Osip Mandelstam, *There Is Nothing that Needs to Be Said*, trans. Jo Ju-gwan, Munhakui sup, 2012.) A world where nothing needs to be said is like death to me, but would the editor have felt something similar? Or had they wanted to memorialise the poet who had been disappeared, in the absence of witnesses, into a world where nothing remained to be said? A world where nothing needs to be said is like death to me, but would the

244   dd's Umbrella

editor have felt something similar? Or had they wanted to memorialise the poet who had been disappeared, in the absence of witnesses, into a world where nothing remained to be said?

Osip Mandelstam was sent to a labour camp in May 1938, during Stalin's Great Purge, after which he vanished without a trace. There are no records to tell us when or how he died. The poetry he wrote had been banned, seized, set aflame, but escaped sinking into complete oblivion thanks to the tireless efforts of his wife, Nadezhda Yakovlevna Mandelstam, who continued to recite and transcribe his poetry from memory. Nadezhda Mandelstam did need words. As do I.

I would like to finish one story in which no one dies. What if, were I to eventually get around to doing so, I titled it 'There Is Nothing that Needs to Be Said'? As the story itself will eventually have to die. As it falls out of use and becomes a story that needs no further telling.

Is this possible?

1.39 p.m.

This is how I record today, the day the revolution is said to have arrived:

That we were all here.

That we sat round this table once everyone was awake, after splashing water on our faces, to share a late breakfast. That Kim Sori had brought over bread soaked in egg milk as a snack for Jung Jinwon, and there was enough for all of us to have toasted and buttered slices of it. That we ate oranges. That we giggled at nothing in particular as we quickly cooked up and wolfed down the food, then sat and had several cups of olive leaf tea. That we discussed how best to talk to a child who had begun to hide away in corners to cry and say things like *Men don't cry*, and wondered and worried about what stories we might and could share with the child in the years to come. That we talked about Sam Smith's coming out and the tense words that were exchanged in Seo Sookyung's class about the universal and the particular. That though we had all noticed the pink hair curlers in the judge's hair that morning as she walked into the court building, none of us had found it in any way remarkable or important enough to comment on, no matter what the media made of it.

Please take your seats.

As the eight Constitutional Court judges entered the main courtroom, we quickly found our own seats in front of the screen. The ruling for Case No. 2016Hun-Na1, Impeachment of the President (Park Geun-hye), began, and suddenly the only sound was of the voice reading out the ruling: Cannot be seen as a violation of... insufficient to prove... it is unclear... no evidence to prove... As the judge continued reading, our faces flushed and our silence grew heavy. Seo Sookyung touched her forehead with the tips of her fingers, I covered my mouth with the hand supporting my chin, Kim Sori rubbed her eyes. The judge began reading the court's decision on whether the state's duty to protect the right to life had been violated.

No one said a thing.

NOTES

d

Chapter 8
'This is only the shallow refuge of the person who does not yet know what he is doing. In fact, the opposite is true.' is from Christopher Alexander, *The Timeless Way of Building*, Oxford University Press, 1979.

There Is Nothing that Needs to Be Said

The title of this section comes from the first line of a poem by Osip Mandelstam as translated by Alex Cigale in 'Anthology of Russian Minimalist and Miniature Poems, Part I, The Silver Age', Offcourse, Issue 41, https://www.albany.edu/offcourse/issue41/cigale_translations4.html. Accessed 29 Oct, 2023.

Chapter 1
'New tablecloth, yellow!...' is a back translation of the Korean translation of Olav H. Hauge's poem 'Ny duk' in 어린 나무의 눈을 털어주다 (Dusting Snow off a Young Tree), trans. Im Seonghi, Springday's Book, 2017.

All quotes from Nietzsche's *The Genealogy of Morals* are in Horace B. Samuel's English translation. Friedrich Nietzsche's *The Genealogy of Morals*, trans. Horace B. Samuel, Boni and Liveright, 1921.

Chapter 3

'the curve of a piece of furniture, or a ship's keel, or the fuselage of an aeroplane… ' is from Antoine de Saint-Exupéry, *Wind, Sand, and Stars*, trans. Lewis Galantière, Reynal & Hitchcock, 1940. All subsequent quotes of Saint-Exupéry in English are from Galantière's translation.

Chapter 5

'here is where my adventure became magical… ' is Galantière's translation, but the rain described as 'miserly' by Galantière is described as 'fiery' in the Korean edition cited in the source text, 인간의 대지 (Land of Men), trans. Kim Yoonjin, Sigongsa, 2014.

Chapter 5

'To live […] is to receive the forms of the life of the sentences that preexist us…' is from Roland Barthes, *The Preparation of the Novel*, trans. Kate Briggs, Columbia University Press, 2010.

Chapter 5

All quotes from Jin-Sung Chun are in Youngjae Josephine Bae's English translation. Jin-Sung Chun, *Imaginary Athens: Urban Space and Memory in Berlin, Tokyo, and Seoul*, trans. Youngjae Josephine Bae, Routledge, 2021.

Chapter 7

'an enormous labour of knowledge...' is from Roland Barthes's *Empire of Signs*, trans. Richard Howard, Hill and Wang 1982.

Chapter 12

'for a last look at peace' and other Zweig quotes are from Stefan Zweig's *The World of Yesterday*, trans. Anthea Bell, Pushkin Press, 2014.

'It happened, therefore it can happen again' is from Primo Levi, *The Drowned and the Saved*, trans. Raymond Rosenthal, Vintage Books, 1980.

Copyright © Hwang Jungeun, 2023

Translation copyright © e. yaewon, 2023

This edition published in the United Kingdom by Tilted Axis Press, 2023.

Originally published in South Korea by Changbi Publishers Inc., 2019.

All rights reserved.

tiltedaxispress.com

The rights of Hwang Jungeun to be identified as the author and e. yaewon as the translator of this work have been asserted in accordance with Section 77 of the Copyright, Designs and Patent Act 1988.

ISBN (paperback): 9781911284949

ISBN (ebook): 9781911284932

A catalogue record for this book is available from the British Library.

Olav H. Hauge: Janglestrå (1980) Copyright © Det Norske Samlaget. Reproduced by permission of Det Norske Samlaget.

Cover Art: Soraya Gilanni Viljoen

Cover Design: Amandine Forest

Art Direction: Soraya Gilanni Viljoen

Typesetting and E-book production: Abbas Jaffary

Editor: Alyea Canada

Copyeditor: Jein Han

Proofreader: Mayada Ibrahim

Acquiring Editor: Deborah Smith

Publishing Assistant: Nguyễn Đỗ Phương Anh

Marketing Manager: Trà My Hickin

Managing Editor: Mayada Ibrahim

Rights Director: Julia Sanches

Publisher: Kristen Vida Alfaro

Made with Hederis

Printed and bound by Clays Ltd, Elcograf S.p.A.

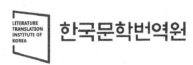

This book is published with the support of the Literature Translation Institute of Korea (LTI Korea)

ABOUT TILTED AXIS PRESS

Tilted Axis publishes mainly work by Asian and African writers, translated into a variety of Englishes. This is an artistic project, for the benefit of readers who would not otherwise have access to the work – including ourselves. We publish what we find personally compelling.

Founded in 2015, we are based in the UK, a state whose former and current imperialism severely impacts writers in the majority world. This position, and those of our individual members, informs our practice, which is also an ongoing exploration into alternatives – to the hierarchisation of certain languages and forms, including forms of translation; to the monoculture of globalisation; to cultural, narrative, and visual stereotypes; to the commercialisation and celebrification of literature and literary translation.

We value the work of translation and translators through fair, transparent pay, public acknowledgement, and respectful communication. We are dedicated to improving access to the industry, through translator mentorships, paid publishing internships, open calls and guest curation.

Our publishing is a work in progress – we are always open to feedback, including constructive criticism, and suggestions for collaborations. We are particularly keen to connect with Black and indigenous translators of Asian and African languages.

tiltedaxispress.com
@TiltedAxisPress